A Wasted Life

A Wasted Life

A Journey in Forgiveness

Marlo Scott

iUniverse, Inc.
New York   Bloomington

iUniverse books may be ordered through booksellers or by contacting:

iUniverse
1663 Liberty Drive
Bloomington, IN 47403
www.iuniverse.com
1-800-Authors (1-800-288-4677)

ISBN: 978-1-4401-7381-3 (sc)
ISBN: 978-1-4401-7383-7 (dj)
ISBN: 978-1-4401-7382-0 (ebook)

Printed in the United States of America

iUniverse rev. date: 10/13/2009

Acknowledgments

My desire to finish this book was just a dream for so long, especially due to an impossibly busy schedule. As I found out, desires can be achieved, and dreams do come true.

The catalysts that changed my thought process from *how*, meaning "how could I ever get this done" to *now*, meaning "now is the time to just do it" were life-changers. Anthony, Rikki, and Beezer were precious souls whose lives were cut short and touched many in their lessons. They inadvertently inspired me to strive for something more. Then, in the middle of my efforts, an era ended with the passing of one of my biggest cheerleaders, my grandmother Edie. Even though I missed her so much, I felt her spirit cheering me on through to the end of my journey. I attained my goal of completing the book and received such tremendous personal satisfaction before I even showed it to a single soul. Stepping outside my comfort zone by sharing it with family and friends was exciting and scary. However, their support and encouragement gave me the push I needed to pursue publication.

I want to thank so many people who helped make this book possible:

Jake and Evan, the most precious gifts that God has ever given me. They are my heart, and they fill my world with smiles, laughter, and an indescribable joy. Being mom to them is the most important job I will ever do, and I am forever grateful to the heavens for giving me this "employment opportunity." I cannot say enough about the perks that come with being their mom. I am privileged to be around these two wonderful human beings. They make everything I do worthwhile.

My husband, John, for his love and support. He watched me endure sleep deprivation, mood swings, and setbacks and never lost confidence in me. I will always be grateful for his sense of humor, strength, and love. He is my soul. I caught me a native, and I'm so glad I did.

Mom and Dad, for their never-ending loyalty and unconditional love. Their advice and encouragement through my life are gifts that can never be repaid. They have shaped me into who I am today, and I thank them for their years of hard work, sacrifice, and worry. They have always stood by me, and together they are my rock.

I feel like the richest woman in the world to have such a great family. I will name a few main players—the Maimones, the Mulieros, the Sendiks, and the Scotts—but there are many supporting characters out there as well.

My coach, Christina, and the friends who couldn't wait until I crossed the finish line, including my Valencia crew.

Luis, for his brilliant artwork. Most notably my proofreaders, including Mary, Lenny, Karen, Aunt Elsie, Aunt Nancy, Aunt Iris, Aunt Jackie, Uncle Ronnie, Gwen, Bill, Michael, Phyllis, Amy, Jaclyn, Liza, Nancy, Brandt, and Randi.

I especially appreciate the authors and professionals who generously gave me so much of their time, valuable advice, and guidance.

Last but not least, Oprah Winfrey, for being a source of information and inspiration to me.

CHAPTER 1

LIFE IS GOOD. As I look around the dinner table and see all the usual family members—Mom, my step-dad, Grandma, aunts, uncles, my husband, Scott, and baby, Jack—I realize I am a lucky girl. My health and my family are all I could ever ask for.

It's an added bonus that I live in Florida, where I get to enjoy beautiful, balmy weather all year long. It's only after living half my life in New York, battling treacherously cold winters, that I can appreciate this. The festive lights, Christmas trimmings, a little wine and some Rosemary Clooney, "Mambo Italiano," all keep the good vibes flowing.

And the abundance of food for our holiday fare is a blessing. Of course it consists of the Italian tradition, the seven fish of Christmas Eve. Growing up predominately Italian-American, I was guilted into never eating meat on Fridays. Christmas Eve was included in this rule, even if it didn't fall on a Friday. Although times have changed from the old days, or even *my* old days, many have kept this tradition, though they might not know the reason for it.

And why seven fish? Some say it signifies seven days of the week, some say it stands for the pilgrimage churches of Rome, while still others say it is for the seven sacraments. Whatever you believe, the seven fish usually include fish salad, anchovies, fried or sandy eel, baccala, fried calamari, clams, and flounder. My family varies this slightly by adding shrimps, scallops or crab-cakes and deleting other items. Whatever the variation, nothing goes to waste in my family. What a bunch of *gavones*.

Even though it sounds like a traditional Italian-American holiday scene, this one always has an added flavor: half my extended family is Jewish. Now, you would never guess this with a glance. Everyone here is loud, uses their hands a lot to express themselves—and rather large noses don't discriminate in this crowd. Sure, there is the aunt who talks about her "mitzvah," but then there is the uncle who tells of the "beatin'" he gave the Off Track Betting guy in the Bronx when things went badly at the races back in the day. In my house, Jewish, Catholic, Italian, whatever—everyone's the same. It is definitely a blended family. The more mixed up things get, the more fun we have.

*   *   *

"Hey, Nina, break out the dessert," Uncle Vinnie shouted to me. "Mah-doan, what you waitin' for, Christmas? Hey, that's a good one, right, kid?" he nudged me in the arm. "'Cause tonight's Christmas Eve."

"Yeah, yeah, you're a funny guy, Uncle Vin," I said.

"You better believe it!" he answered.

Uncle Vinnie answered everything with "You better believe it." That was his mantra. I think he got it from my grandmother on my mother's side, whom I affectionately called "Crazy Nana" because she was. That was one of her favorite lines, along with, "I'll fix you!" and "Go figure." She was a beautiful Irish woman who was married to my deceased grandfather, a full-blooded Italian from off the boat.

"*Aspetto*, keep your shirt on," my mother, Caroline, said. "I'll bring it out after I dance with my other brother."

Mom liked to dance with Uncle Mario. Her specialty looked like a combination of the bump and the "Elaine," from *Seinfeld*. Uncle Mario swore that her hips were magical, and that dancing actually helped his bad hip feel better. After every dance he would say, "I'm feelin' no pain." The fact that he was a habitual pot-smoker might have something to do with that.

My step-dad, Harry, was an extremely good-natured soul. I called him Dad because to me he embodied what a dad should be. He loved to watch my mother, or any of us for that matter, have a great time. I think it made his heart happy when we were all happy.

As "Lazy Mary" began and Uncle Mario and Mom started dancing in the living room, Harry shouted, "Well here they are, ladies and gentlemen, couple number one!"

Everyone got up and circled them like a mosh-pit. Age did not matter. The young and old were up, clapping, laughing, and shouting, perma-smiles plastered on their faces. Everyone was having so much fun. I was totally in the moment.

The phone rang. My mother stopped dancing to answer it as I took her place on the dance floor. A moment later she called my name, crooked a finger and bade me to come over. She had a weird look in her eye.

"Nina, ah … it's your father."

As she handed me the phone, I knew this call would change everything.

"Hello. You there, Nina?"

"Oh, yeah. Hi. How are you?" I said nervously.

At this point, I was reeling. Everyone around me was having a rollicking good time, and suddenly I was on another planet. I had not heard from Joey, who called himself my father, in five years. In recent years I'd had a hard time referring to him as "Dad" and almost always thought of him by his name. His voice, gruff with a thick New York accent, was weaker than I remembered. He sounded like a nervous suitor trying to ask for a date. This was very awkward.

"You know it's Christmas, and I, uh, got to thinkin', it might be nice to call. You know, your aunt is here, my sista, and she kept breakin' my balls about you, how we should talk. Anyway, how you doin'?"

"I'm good," I said matter-of-factly. There was a long pause before I could say anything else. "You know you have a grandson who is almost one. Anyway, do you need anything? Is that why you're calling?"

I just wanted to cut to the chase. You have to understand, this was a man who had not worked for a very long time and was always on the take. He had even bankrupted his second wife, as he had one foot out the door and a girlfriend on the side. When my grandfather died, Joey was in dire straits and took all the money Grandpa left for him and me. He thought nothing of taking money from my aunt, his sister, who was taking care of their elderly, sick mother. I wasn't upset about the money, because I never had any, so I didn't miss it. I was just appalled at my father's greed and lack of respect.

I was disgusted to think I was walking around with his genes. Now to top it off, he told me it was because my aunt was "breakin' balls" that he was calling. After I cooled off for a minute I allowed myself to give him a little bit of a break. After all, he did make the phone call.

"No, no I don't need anything," Joey said. His voice was low and humble now.

"You know, a lot of time has gone by. It's a shame," I said scolding but evenly.

"I know, but you could've picked up a phone, too, you know, Neen. I don't fuckin' know why things happened this way. I didn't think you wanted to fuckin' talk to me. What do I know? It was a fuckin' waste, I know."

The talk could get rough with Joey. I didn't take any offense to his vulgar language even after all this time. That was always his way. He had a Sylvester Stallone sort of drawl but always came off like Robert De Niro in *Goodfellas*. That was on a good day. On a bad day, when he was really angry, his demeanor was more like Tony Montana in *Scarface*.

"Anyway, how are you feeling?" I asked.

"Good, good, except I walk with a cane now, but I still got the big guns," he laughed.

I chuckled with him at that one. He had always worked out. His nineteen-inch biceps were his pride and joy. I wouldn't be surprised if he had named them. But it was clear he was broken down at this point. After years of polluting his body with alcohol and drugs—and many bar fights and accidents later—it had only been a matter of time before he would break down physically.

"You getting around okay?" I asked.

"I'm in a different apartment now," he answered. "You know, *cosi-cosi*, so-so. I'm still in the Bronx, not a very good neighborhood, though. But I'm with Charo, and her father has a place downstairs from me, so when I get sick of her I can send her down to him. You know what I mean, *capisce*?"

When he said *"capisce"* it was always rhetorical.

My aunt Joanne, his sister, was one of my favorite people. She'd been giving me the 411 on Joey's life over the years, sometimes details I could've done without. Charo was Joey's "girlfriend." Actually, I didn't know what she was. I didn't even know if she was a *she*.

Joey met Charo while he was involved with someone else, and she remained a secret for a while. I met her five years ago in a social club near his apartment across from the Bronx Zoo, right before Joey and I stopped talking. I was not married yet, and it had been a while since I had seen him. I remembered that I was still mad at him for the embarrassing way he treated me when I introduced him to Scott.

*   *   *

During his first encounter with Scott I was so excited to show Joey that I was a "big girl," making big decisions, and had found a partner for life. Not to mention, I wanted Scott to meet this man who had been a big part of my life and who I had told Scott so much about.

When Scott and I got there, Joey laughed at us and said we looked like Ken and Barbie. He thought it was hysterical that Scott is so tall while I am so short. Well, hello, the apple doesn't fall far from the tree. Joey is vertically challenged and has a raging Napoleonic complex— short man's syndrome. Never give Joey a challenge, no matter how big or strong you are. It was like his whole life was about proving himself.

Joey wanted to know about Scott's nationality. He has an all-American look and a generic last name, Evans. Scott is Italian but also is a pot-pourri of nationalities from his father's side. Joey kept asking Scott what he bench pressed and basically told him he could bench more. He even asked Scott if he wanted to see his rifle. At least he was polite and asked; he never bothered to ask my other suitors in the past. If he was in the mood to throw down the guns, he just did it.

So a couple of months after that fiasco of Scott meeting Joey, I was a little apprehensive about seeing Joey again, much less meeting this very colorful person in his life. It was five years ago but I will never forget meeting Charo.

*   *   *

When I got to New York, my aunt Joanne, who was nice enough to drive us to the Bronx, told Scott and me that there was no elevator at Joey's apartment, so we walked up a narrow flight of stairs.

I knocked on the door anxiously. When there was no answer, Aunt Joanne pulled out a spare key she had in case of emergencies and let us in. No one was there, so we waited ... and waited. After a while, she decided to run over to the social club around the block where Joey liked to hang out. Since he didn't have a cell phone then, this was the best way she could think of to find him.

Now, it was typical for Joey to be late, but he knew we were coming, so what was the problem? After fifteen minutes, Aunt Joanne called my cell phone and said she would come get us to meet Joey at the social club. So she got us, locked up the apartment, and we walked. It was rainy, and Scott and I followed her down the old, dingy street. There was a lot of trash on the sidewalk and spilling into the streets. The sidewalks were full of bumps and cracks.

The concept of the social club really had its heyday in the 50s, 60s, and 70s, when "connected" members of society dominated the streets in this neck of the woods. Usually, Italian men with mob ties would come to these places to hang out, "shoot the shit," play cards, and drink espresso or other beverages of choice. These places, which were usually just neighborhood houses featuring one big, open room with a wooden bar and a couple of rickety card tables and chairs, were always open. There was always someone tending the bar, unofficially. In this case, it was Charo.

My aunt wanted us to quicken our pace, since she knew there were some mean-looking neighborhood dogs close by. I guess she had a near miss with one on her first trip over here. After stepping over dog poop and avoiding tripping on cracks and holes in the sidewalks, we made it to a wrought-iron gate at the front of the fence. The houses were so close together they looked like they were connected. They all had chain-link fences running around the front.

At that point my aunt felt the need to mention, yet again, not to get alarmed when Scott and I meet Charo. I thought, *How bad could she be?*

We got to an old, wooden door, and upon opening it, I saw Joey sitting at a table, smoking a cigarette, as calm as could be. No apology for making us wait or not being where he said he would be. He shot us a look as if to say, "What took you so long?"

"A, oh! Hey, Neen, you finally made it. How ya doin', Scott? Come, sit. Youz want anything to drink?" he asked nervously.

Scott asked for water. By the looks of the place, I would be surprised if they even had running water. As for me, I was not going to have anything.

We all sat, and as Joey puffed on his cigarette, he looked me up and down appraisingly and slightly nodding his head as if to say "yes."

"My God, you are a looker," he finally concluded. "I mean, for Christ's sakes, you're a woman. And when did you get that body? You been in the gym like your old man, I can tell. You look good, kid."

He was always going to call me "kid." I think it was his way of keeping me in my place, rather than an endearment. He had a way of always making me feel like an awkward little girl, no matter what I was saying or doing. I could have been delivering a speech to the United Nations and he still would say something like, "You did good, kid" and brush his hand across my nose.

"You gettin' bags under your eyes, though," he said. "What, you not gettin' any sleep? Scott keepin' you awake at night?"

I wasn't sure if he was serious so I answered him quickly. "No, it's a family trait. You should look in the mirror." I laughed.

It was true. He and I look so much alike. If I have bags, I've probably inherited them from him. I also have his full lips, prominent nose, brown eyes, and thick brown hair. The only differences are that my eyes are big and my smile is wide, just like my mom. People say I sound just like her too. And my hair is long, maybe too long now that I'm a mom. Nevertheless, I am a female version of Joey. He is a good-looking man, I just don't know if the features I inherited from him translate into prettiness as a girl. I'd like to think I'm fairly attractive. In my experience, I have never really had to run after the opposite sex. Therefore, I think it's safe to say I'm easy on the eyes, minus the bags.

Just then I saw something that shocked me, a mystery I would never unlock. Someone who appeared to be a woman came strutting out of the bathroom. But this was no ordinary person. She was like a Spanish version of RuPaul. Let's start with her get-up. She had on a low-cut, red, polyester mini-dress. Her boobs were not huge, but they were stuffed into a tight-fitting bra that pushed them out like a display shelf. She wore fishnet stockings with thigh-high, vinyl, high-heeled boots, which, I found out later, were her signature. She was adorned with big hoop earrings and cheap, dollar-store bangles on each wrist, all different colors.

"*Ay Dios mio*, Joey, is thees yauw dauwta?" Charo exclaimed with a Spanish, south Bronx accent. "She beauteeful!"

Joey got up and made the introductions. At this point I must've resembled a Steamboat Willie cartoon where Willie sees trouble coming and his eyes bug out and his tongue flops to the ground. After I rolled my tongue up off the floor, I tried to be gracious and say hello. In my peripheral vision, I could see Scott's expression of disbelief. I was afraid to catch his eye for fear he would crack up.

I know this sounds mean, but Charo was truly unlike anything I had ever seen, and I couldn't believe she was dating my father. We stood up, and she immediately came up to me for a hug. As she drew me in, I anticipated a kiss. I quickly turned and gave her my cheek. It was an involuntary reaction. Once I got close to her face, something in my brain wouldn't let me keep looking, kind of like when you try to stare at the sun.

She had what can only be described as a Batman-like mask of black eyeliner around her eyes. It started on the bridge of her nose and extended out to her temples on both sides. It was drawn so thickly that it extended all the way up to where eyebrows should have been. Either she had lost the ability to grow eyebrows or she had shaved them off. Instead, she drew them, also in black, up on her forehead. She also wore fake eyelashes and dark red lipstick. Her blush was so dark it looked like someone had punched her in the cheeks.

As my head turned, my upper body arched back in an effort to avoid her hair, which took on a life of its own. It was definitely a wig, blonde and teased, at least a foot high. The women of the B-52's, even with their exaggerated beehive hairdos, had nothing on Charo. I really had never seen anything like this. Even when I was younger and Joey would take me through Harlem or the Bronx on our way to the City and I would spot prostitutes on the street, they still didn't look as flamboyant as Charo.

"Oh, and ees thees you fiancé?" she said, looking at me but referring to Scott.

Then she turned to him, and I hoped he would hold it together and try not to make any crazy-looking faces as she approached him.

"Oh ju gorgeous," she said to Scott. "Baby, Joey, look how gorgeous he ees. They so beauteeful together, right?"

"Right, right, get us some drinks, hon," Joey barked.

He looked at us as if to say, "Yeah what can I do." But I thought, *You could get the hell out of here, that's what you could do.* I wouldn't dare say that, though.

"She's cute, huh?" Joey said.

I didn't know if this was a trick question or if I was even supposed to answer. At this point, I thought I could communicate with him and get real. I made eye contact with Joey and said in a low voice, "Is this real, are you kidding? What's with the outfit?"

"I know she's a bit much," Joey explained. "It's her style. But you got to get to know her. She's a pisser."

What I wanted to know was whether she peed standing up or sitting down, but I thought that would be a little disrespectful, plus she was coming up to our table. She looked like a drag queen to me.

"So Joey keeps you waiting," Charo said in a singsong voice. "Poor babies. Don't feel bad, sweeties; he always keeps me waiting too. He's a bad bo-oy."

I was sickened as they chuckled together. I just had to sit back and watch the show. I couldn't believe what I was seeing. I was actually embarrassed for Joey. Had he forgotten that he used to be "the man"? If confidence counted for anything, he had it to an obnoxious degree. He exuded so much confidence that gorgeous women always wanted to be by his side, even at his lowest points of depression. He was a master at putting on a show no matter how he was feeling inside.

But now I just didn't know if he was suffering from dementia instead. Or maybe he was going blind. Either way, I wanted to stand up and scream. I thought maybe this was a joke and I was being "punked." At one point I wanted to cry, thinking I was dragging Scott into this circus of my family life. What had he done to deserve this? Then I got a grip and realized this was Joey's life and if he was happy, so be it. I just found it unbelievable that he could be happy this way.

*   *   *

So as my mind wandered back to the conversation at hand on this balmy Christmas Eve in Florida, I realized this time Joey wanted some sort of answer from me when he said *capisce*.

"Yo … hello! Neen, ya there? Joey barked.

"Yeah, yeah, Jesus, I'm sorry. I was listening. I just didn't realize you needed a response."

"Yeah don't get cute," he quipped.

In his vernacular, when Joey said "cute," he wasn't referring to someone's appearance. It was more in reference to being a wiseass. I think he thought the whole world was one big wiseass. I mean, sometimes he acted as if everyone was out to get him. So whenever I said anything half-jokingly, he said I was being cute. That usually prompted his hand to go up, as if to say a backhand would be coming if I kept it up. The good news for me is that I was a girl. If I were a guy, odds are that backhand would have made contact with me, often.

At this point, I realized my relatives were looking at me and giving me the "what gives" sign. My mom had worn a concerned expression while she was trying to listen to our conversation.

"Hey, how's the weather down there, Nina?" Joey asked.

"It's really great this time of year. Florida winters are mild."

"Yeah, I always wanted to move there, he said." "It's fuckin' freezing here. Well, what ya gonna do."

I felt that was my cue to wrap up the call, but it was awkward. It was like he wanted to stay on the phone but had nothing to say. I made it easy for him.

"Well, I got to go. Everyone is looking at me and waiting for me to break out the dessert and limoncellos. Will we speak again?"

"Yeah, yeah, this was good," he said. "Can I call next week?"

That's never going to happen. "Of course. I hope to hear from you."

It was all I could say. I didn't want to seem overly eager, and I definitely didn't want to get my hopes up. Joey had disappointed me hundreds of times before.

But there seemed to be something different about his voice. I felt as though he was getting old. Of course we all get o*lder*, but he actually sounded old. I almost felt a pang of sadness for him. I wondered how he was doing, really.

CHAPTER 2

I WAS NEVER YOUR STEREOTYPICAL child of divorced parents. The situation never became about me. Whenever the subject of divorce came up on television or in the paper, it was always about the child. Concern for, how to raise, how to break the news to, how to not spoil, how to share … *the child*.

In my case, Joey was always the child. He suffered from manic depression. When he was in a good mood, everything was great. He had everyone join the happy high road with him. Everyone was included in his party. But when he was angry, everyone had better get out of the way.

One of my earliest memories of his rage came when I was four years old and my parents were still together. I was awakened from a deep sleep to hear him arguing with my mother. This was not unusual. This time, however, he was graphically describing what he would do to her if she didn't stop questioning him when he returned from his nights on the town. He was drunk, but not really slurring his words. He may have been high, too, but "drunk" was the only word I knew at such a young age. My mother always yelled at him for being "piss drunk."

Something about this fight scared me, and I got out of my bed. I heard a big commotion in the hallway outside my room, then it seemed to move a little farther away. I heard a lot of banging into the wall, as if someone were being pushed. None of that made me think twice about leaving the safety of my room. I just wanted someone to hold me and tell me things would be okay, so I grabbed my doll and opened my door. I hoped one of them would see me and stop fighting instantly, but as I rounded the corner, a can of some beverage came flying at my body, and then another at my head. I screamed, and Joey walked away cursing.

"Son of a bitch. Put this kid to bed, will ya? This is some mothafuckin' bullshit I gotta come home to." He threw his hands up as if he was annoyed that I ruined a perfectly good fight.

My mother screamed in horror to think one of those cans could have made contact with my little body. She ran to me to examine and comfort me. She hugged me tightly and carried me back to bed, apologizing and sobbing.

In a way, I was lucky, because Joey gave me a major education in the school of life. It helped prepare me for the world outside my door.

*   *   *

In 1977, lots was going on in the world and in New York City. The economy was on a downward spiral, everyone was complaining about the future of the City, and the world outside my home seemed dirty. When adults would talk around me, I always heard second-hand stories about crazy nights out on the town. Underground music was starting to hit the streets. Studio 54 was the hot place to be—and speaking of hot, we had a major blackout that summer. July 13 would become known as the "night the lights went out." That night I didn't get to turn on the A/C unit perched in my window. It was miserably hot.

But I did get to learn about terror that night. Sure, Joey had taught me my fair share, but this was nightmarish, paralyzing fear. In fact, *TIME Magazine* referred to that evening as "the night of terror." You see, it was also "the summer of Sam." Otherwise known as David Berkowitz, the Son of Sam was a serial killer who preyed on young girls. Girls older than I was, but I was still scared. I was seven years old and back then, adults didn't tell kids everything the way they do now, so I could only gather information from bits and pieces of grown-up conversations.

"I attended the same science class as this lunatic," one of my uncles said just a couple of weeks prior to this terrifying night. "This psychopath killed one of my ex-girlfriends. I'll never forget it, and I'll never forgive him."

It was all he could talk about, and it definitely had an impact on me. I didn't need to watch the evening news; I heard everything I needed to know from the adults. What I heard scared me so much that at night I would stay up for fear the Son of Sam was lurking in the trees outside my quaint, two-story, two-family home in Yonkers. We lived on the first floor, with a small set of stairs past our stoop leading right to the street. I would sit in my bed and study the shadows on my wall to make sure no one was hiding in the bushes just beyond my window.

When the blackout hit that night, I worried even more, because we had to keep the windows open. Despite the sweltering heat, I kept getting shivers through my body at the thought of "Sam" showing up.

And things were far worse outside. From what I heard on the battery-powered radio in the kitchen, it seemed as if the whole city was going crazy. From Brooklyn to the Bronx and all points in between, people were looting. Would these crazies hit my town next? The reporter was trying to be heard over the sound of bottles breaking and shots being fired. Everyone was going nuts. Buildings were being set ablaze. Would my house be next? I shut my eyes as tightly as I could and prayed for sleep. I felt like Dorothy from *The Wizard of Oz*: I just wanted to click my heels and get my normal chaos back.

One night, when the commotion was over, the lights were back on, and Sam was in jail, Joey wanted to take my mom and me to a dinner party at Nonna's house. Nonna was his mother, a docile, fragile woman. She and Joey had a very rocky start. As a child, Joey was no picnic in the park. For a time his mother sent him to live with one of his aunts.

When I was a little girl, Joey and Nonna got along fine, and he was always respectful. I don't think she really knew about his dark side, no matter how crazy he got around her. As many mothers did back then, she just turned a blind eye to most of his antics. Whenever my mother complained to her about Joey, Nonna would just respond casually.

"What ya gonna do?" she'd say to my mother. "It is what it is."

It was an answer that suggested, "Just throw in the towel and deal with it." And that's just what Mom did for a little while.

Now, I don't remember much about this party, just that there was a lot of food, more booze, and lots of noise. Joey's family was extremely boisterous, and expletives were flying. It didn't matter that my young cousins and I were present. None of the adults curtailed any of their bad behavior for our sake, ever. Basically we were told, "Do as I say, not as I do."

When Nonna was done playing cards, she just sat back in her reclining chair. She never played hostess at any gathering at her house. Parties simply seemed to form and take on a life of their own at Nonna and Grandpa Nunzio's house.

Grandpa Nunzio was a real character. He wore thick black glasses and started the day with Scotch on the rocks. He always smelled of alcohol. He had that stereotypically Irish drinker's nose, big and red, but he was full-blooded Sicilian, right off the boat. He had served in World War II, and that boozer nose was his merit badge. He had become a successful insurance salesman who told jokes and was always sarcastic. He got a kick out of his grandkids but only in small doses. If any of us were around for an extended period of time he usually just tolerated our presence and chose to talk politics with our fathers in the kitchen.

He had less than endearing little Italian nicknames for us all, but mine was the least endearing. He would call me *facia brut*, which means "ugly face." That did lots for my self-esteem as a little girl, but I would just shrug it off after my mother reassured me it was not true.

However, Grandpa Nunzio did occasionally share a tender tradition with me. While we sat at the kitchen table, he would sing to me in a cracking, smoker's voice;

"Mama's little baby loves shortnin', shortnin',
Mama's little baby loves shortnin' bread."

He said that oftentimes his mother used to sing that to him when he was a little boy. That song was all the alone time he ever gave me.

In general, Nonna was usually the only other female in the kitchen with Grandpa, and she would just sit and listen quietly, nodding her head occasionally.

Grandpa Nunzio had a very stern, deep voice, and when he raised it people would stop talking and pay attention. Everyone did except Joey. He seemed to have a way of egging Grandpa Nunzio on. I felt as though every time we were there, Joey would leave in an argument with somebody, mostly Grandpa. This dinner party was no exception.

"What the fuck you talking about?" Joey shouted at Grandpa. "Fuhgeddaboutit."

Sometimes, when Joey would start his tirade, it wasn't clear whether he was just getting loud to get attention or if he was really angry.

"You think I'm gonna take that from you here? You think I need a handout from you? That I got *oogats* [nothing]?" His voice grew louder with each phrase. "You tryin' to insult me in front of my fuckin' family? Show off what a big man you are in front of my wife and kid?"

"Jesus, Joey, calm down," Grandpa yelled back. "It's just a gesture, for the kid."

"I don't need you or anybody else to make no fuckin' gesture," Joey said. "You know your ass would never offer shit unless there was a crowd of people to see you do it."

With those words, everyone got still. One of the uncles tried to calm Joey. Two seconds later, Joey was yelling at him and storming out of the door. My mother quickly grabbed our coats, and we left without proper good-byes. As she raced down the front steps, she had tears in her eyes. I could hear the commotion inside.

All Joey's aunts and uncles were yelling, and Aunt Joanne came out pleading with us not to go. It was a useless effort. Joey was honking the horn and slamming his fists on the steering wheel. He rolled down the window and screamed at us.

"Get in the fuckin' car, now!"

We got in and arrived home safely, thanks be to God.

CHAPTER 3

DRIVING IN THE CAR WITH Joey was always an adventure. It was amazing I was even alive to talk about it. In the '70s, there were no seatbelt laws or rules about where children should sit in a car. So there I would be, in the front or back seat, sans seat belt, driven by a man who had been drinking way too much and was usually pissed off.

Sometimes when we started out, everything was wonderful. Joey would seem as happy as could be. Most of the time, if he had music and cigarettes while driving his fancy Caddy, then he was set.

He was an avid music lover. His tastes included rock, country, Latin, old standards, you name it. He loved Tony Bennett, but also The Beatles. He loved Eric Clapton, but also Willie Nelson.

And just as his musical likes varied, so did his looks. Sometimes he wore a cowboy hat, other times his hair was slicked back and he would wear a guinea-T, and still other times he looked ready to take off on a Harley. However, he almost always wore cowboy boots. With slacks or jeans, it didn't matter; he always had on a pair of the finest snakeskin boots. I think he thought boots gave him height while still looking masculine. The only time he didn't wear them was when he was lifting weights. Then he went barefoot or wore flip-flops.

I knew he was in a good mood if he was waiting in the car for us and had the stereo blasting and was wearing his favorite boots. But even that couldn't predict how his mood would stay.

One weekend night my mother, Joey, and I were coming back from a movie theater. We were just cruising, when all of a sudden a car cut in front of us and sped through the yellow light.

"Son of a bitch! That mothafucka!" Joey shouted as we got caught at red.

"Oh Joey, please, please calm down," my mother said. She gasped and moaned as if in physical pain while Joey slammed on the brakes.

The car that cut us off was approaching a hill up ahead, and the driver got caught at that red light. Joey jumped out of our car and rushed to the trunk.

"What are you doing? Please stop!" my mother said. "Please, Joey, please. Don't do this with Nina in the car. I'm beggin' you."

Joey had reached into the trunk and grabbed a rifle. Her hands covered her face in horror at what she saw. Mom was crying wildly at this point. Joey ignored everything. He saw red. He started running up the hill, past oncoming traffic, shooting at the car that had cut us off.

My body quivered with every shot. My mother just turned to me, pinning me with a serious look, and told me to cover my eyes. I couldn't, though. I was frozen in the moment. It was as if there were no other cars on the road but us and that car Joey was shooting at.

When our light turned green, cars started honking and swerving to go around us. My mother was sobbing and twitching. She was panicking in the passenger seat. We saw Joey running and shooting even as the car's driver spun its tires to race through the light to escape the madman Joey. He stood on top of the hill, partially illuminated by the streetlights. Then he turned and started walking back to us.

Mom was sobbing. I was too, but only inside my mind. On the outside, my face was frozen.

Joey slammed the trunk shut and got in the car. "You believe that mothafucka?" he asked matter-of-factly, then looked at my mother. "Yo Caroline, quit ya cryin'. The guy deserved a beatin'. He's lucky he's not dead right now."

I could not believe what had just occurred. I was starting to realize no one I knew had to witness things like this. This was not normal behavior for most people. I had no one I could talk to about it. So life went on.

Shortly after that incident, Mom and Joey split up. Mom and I moved to a simple, two-bedroom apartment. For a while, things got weirder. One minute Joey would be staying over, the next minute he'd be gone. They would date one day; the next day they were at each other's throats again. This went on for a while, and all while they dated other people.

My mother knew Joey had been seeing someone else for years. He pretty much kept his girlfriend, Patti, away from me, but he had mentioned her name to me, probably in preparation for a future meeting.

On one occasion, Joey had just dropped me back at my mom's apartment after a long day in the city together, and my mother decided to let him have it. If something was bothering her, she usually curtailed her anger for the time Joey and I were together, because she didn't want to upset him while I was in his care.

"How dare you pick up our daughter with that tramp bitch's underwear in the backseat!" Mom shouted over the phone to Joey. "Do you think I'm stupid?"

"Of course he does," Crazy Nana chimed in like a spokesperson for her daughter. She lived with us most of the time and always listened to everyone's conversations and then gave her two cents, as if she was an invited third party. Like it or not, she was going to provide her commentary.

"This has been going on with you and her for years," Mom's voice rose shrilly. "I hope you drop dead!" She slammed down the phone and started bawling.

"It's disgusting, he's disgusting," Crazy Nana mumbled, still stuck on the underwear situation. She loved to stand in a Marlene Dietrich pose, holding a cigarette, and tell people what they should be doing.

"What, do ya think that underwear trick was an accident? That was for your benefit, Caroline. I wouldn't give him the time of day. The next time he would see me is never."

Crazy Nana always made so much sense—or should I say non-sense.

I was sure my mother would have loved to have nothing to do with Joey ever again, but I stood in her way. Of course she had to see him when it came to things concerning me. When he came to pick me up for the day or weekend, my mom would wait with me and was always there to give me a big hug and kiss good-bye. It must have killed her inside to let me go with him.

One day Joey found a way to blow off some steam that caused another argument. He bought a motorcycle. He chose a Harley

Davidson Fat Boy, possibly a little too big for his size, but he didn't care. He was a pit bull: a small dog with ferocious strength and temperament. He loved to ride. He often rode after drinking in the bar. He didn't even want to drive his Cadillac anymore. He was addicted to his bike. He had a very tedious and strenuous job as an air traffic controller. He said riding his motorcycle to and from work, an hour away, relaxed him.

One night after working a double, he went to a local watering hole and knocked a few back with his boys. This was a point when he and Mom were "on again," so he got on his Harley and headed home to Mom and me.

I was asleep, but I remember waking up in the middle of the night. I could hear something that sounded like it was coming from the hallway of our apartment building, but I couldn't quite make out the sound. I tiptoed out to the front of our apartment and was about to put my ear up to the door for a better listen, when all of a sudden there was whimpering and scratching at the door. I jumped back. I immediately thought a cat must have run into the building and be searching for food or a way to get out. The sounds were scary to me.

Just then my mother came up behind me. She had a listen and ordered me back to my room. Reluctantly, I went back. I wanted to know what was out there, and I was concerned for my mother, since I knew she was about to open the door. The minute she opened it, she shrieked and screamed Joey's name.

She immediately screamed out to me to stay in my room with the door closed. I was afraid, but since I wanted to know what was going on, I kept my door open a crack so I could peek out with one eye.

Mom was racing around the apartment in search of the telephone. She called for an ambulance, then immediately dropped the phone to get back to Joey. I saw her trying to drag him into our foyer. He was red and unable to talk, just kind of moaning. I could see only his head and shoulders on the floor as she tried to get the rest of his body inside. Now *her* clothes were turning red. As I saw more of his body, I realized the red all over was blood. I was groggy, but now I was waking up and freaking out. I was only eight years old but I was intuitive enough to know something was terribly wrong.

My mother knelt down beside him and put a wet cloth on his head and laid towels over his wounds. As she asked questions about what happened, he muttered responses. She'd listen, only interrupting to soothe him. Later, I found out what happened.

Joey would recall that when he left the bar in the middle of the night, after having a few too many, he jumped on his motorcycle and headed to his apartment which was one exit away from where we were living. It was rainy, and he decided to take back roads instead of the highways. He was going faster than he should have, but wanted to get to home to go to sleep. Furthermore, he could go faster on the back roads, with less chance of meeting cops and other cars. Just as he approached our exit, his tires caught some wet gravel. He started to swerve. He overcompensated to avoid the gravel and lost control of the bike. Joey laid it down and went for the ride. The motorcycle was in charge.

"The only thing I know is that when I hit the ground, I immediately felt my side pop," Joey said. "It felt like I was being stabbed."

He broke some ribs. Then came his leg. He said he could feel his leg grinding against the road but didn't know which pain was worse—that or the burning, heavy metal of the bike on top of his leg. His leg was trapped and crushed. He managed to keep his head up most of the time but he had major road rash all over as his clothes peeled away onto the pavement, leaving his skin exposed.

What he did next was quite unbelievable and probably only possible because he was partially numb from the alcohol he had consumed. He said after realizing that his leg was broken, he started to crawl to our apartment. It was a couple of miles away but still closer than where he was living. He said he stopped many times but knew if he could just get to us he would be okay. Too bad there were no cell phones in those days. He was lucky he didn't get run over. I guess things could've been much worse if this hadn't happened during the middle of the night when there were hardly any cars on the road. On the other hand if it had happened in the day there probably would have been more people around to help him.

I thought it was quite incredible that Joey didn't bleed to death, considering all his injuries. It turned out he had a punctured lung, a couple of broken ribs, and a severely broken leg. He had too many scrapes and burn marks to mention. He said he almost gave up when he knew he had to pry open the door to the building. He was on the verge of passing out. He dragged himself into our building and army-crawled to our door. Lucky for him, we lived on the first floor.

Once the ambulance came, I knew I wouldn't see him again for a while.

CHAPTER 4

JOEY WAS IN THE HOSPITAL for days. This wasn't the first time; accidents and bar fights had sent him there before. The problem for him this time was that he had broken this same leg before. When he was admitted, he had no feeling in his leg. When he told us about it later, he said he heard doctors talking over him about possible amputation. He couldn't speak at the time, but he said in his head he felt like screaming out, "No, please don't take my leg! Take my fuckin' life if you have to do that."

The next day or so, when he was coherent, he said things really turned around.

"Doc, doc, get the hell over here right now," Joey screamed as the doctor stood in the hallway outside his hospital room.

"Good morning, Mr. Martino, how are you today?" the good doctor asked.

"Cut the small talk, doc," he quipped. "Do what you gotta do and do it! Get this leg off. I can't stand the fuckin' pain, not a minute longer, 'scuse my French." Joey was spitting as he spoke. He was delirious from the pain.

"Mr. Martino, I'm setting you up with a drip right now that should take the edge off," explained the doctor. "You have been through a horrific experience, and we're doing everything we can for you."

"Ahhh, don't touch me, this is killin' me," Joey screamed as the doctor examined the leg. "Take it off, just take it off."

"Uh oh, no sir. Actually, I'm glad to see you in this much pain," the doctor said with a smile. "This is good news for you. It means you have lots of feeling in the leg. The nerve endings are working. We are putting you back together, and you will be good as new in no time. I will check in with you later. For now, you're in good hands."

"Wait, doc! What the fuck! You gotta be kiddin' me."

Joey's tirade continued for a couple more minutes, until his medications started to take effect. Nurses kept peeking out from behind their posts, looking to see who was cursing so much. Joey couldn't have cared less. His road to recovery was just beginning, and it wouldn't be an easy one. And finally he drifted off to sleep again.

My mother let Joey stay with us for a while until he could get up and around again. The crazy thing was that he purchased another motorcycle and rode it, even with the cast. His ribs and cuts and bruises healed, but the leg had a long way to go. One day, as I peeked in my mother's bedroom to get a look at Joey's cast, he called me in.

"It's okay, Nina, come in," he said.

I had never seen anyone in a cast up close. It was weird to me, but I was interested all the same.

"Hi, Daddy. Are you in pain today?" I asked.

He had just gotten out of the shower and was partially dressed. He smelled like Old Spice. It was a scent I would always associate with him. His leg was wrapped in a plastic bag to keep the cast dry. However, today he said he wanted to take the cast off, even though he didn't have the doctor's permission.

"Grab me that shoe horn, will ya?" he asked.

As he grabbed it from me, he immediately snaked it down in between the cast and his leg and started wiggling it back and forth.

"Uggghh, it feels so good. My leg is so itchy, what a relief," he sighed. "You know what I really gotta do? I gotta take this crap off. Neen, do me a favor and close the door. I don't want your mother to see this."

"If you don't want Mommy to see this, then why are you doing it?"

"'Cause your mother wouldn't approve," he answered. "You see, she plays by the rules, and I don't. You need to be like her, not me. Remember that," Joey explained.

"The doc told me not to do this, but I don't care. I need to let the leg breathe a little." He sat on the edge of the bed, cracked the cast, and began unraveling the dressing.

"Why are you showing me this?" I asked.

"For educational purposes," he answered in a smart-ass tone.

All of a sudden the cast was off and his leg was free. His knee just cleared the edge of the bed. As soon as the cast was off, he grabbed a stool and propped it underneath the upper part of his calf. Just then, something unnatural happened. His leg bent from the mid part of the bottom half of his leg, between the knee and ankle and just underneath the calf.

"Eeewww, Daddy!" I ran screaming out of the room. I could hear him laughing. Was this funny? Wasn't he in pain? My mother would have a field day with this once she heard what happened. I definitely would never get the image of what I saw out of my head. It was just plain gross.

When all was said and done, he bounced back, and I guess the whole experience reaffirmed my view of him as superhuman. He sometimes seemed mammoth to me, even though he was small in stature. People were afraid of him. I mistook this for power, so it was exciting to be around him. I could see how my mother was attracted to him. He was powerful and good-looking. He had wavy, dark brown hair with chestnut eyes, and a strong, chiseled jaw with a prominent Roman nose. His body was just as chiseled. He had muscles all day. He was a superb specimen; his only drawback physically was his height. He was hot and a bad boy, and my mother married him. Being the daughter of the bad boy, what I learned was this: you should *never marry the bad boy.*

Joey loved to take me out to dinner, and he always took me places where he got red-carpet treatment, almost always in Little Italy or the Bronx. I was a little kid from Yonkers, but when I went out to dinner with my dad, I ate like the Queen of England.

At Gino's, a restaurant in the Bronx, I always heard stories about the old days. It was like a history lesson. First, Joey would make his way through the crowded and smoky bar with a hand up as a gesture to say hi or maybe show off his pinky ring, I don't know. Everyone knew him there. Usually there was a baseball or football game on the small corner television. I always thought it was snowing wherever the game was because the reception was so poor. Occasionally, if a very important person was there, Joey would stop and actually shake a hand. Tony "Bo" Pastorelli was Joey's partner in crime, literally, and if he was there

I knew we wouldn't be going anywhere for a long while. I also knew I would not be talking as long as he was sitting with us.

Tony Bo was very daunting. He always wore a suit, and he'd usually start the conversation with "You take care a that thing we talked about?" Joey would usually reply with "Fuhgeddaboutit, piece a cake. Fuckin' guy … that strunze." Then they would laugh and start talking in code, as if I were the FBI or something. It was all so boring to me. I later found out that the "bow" in Tony Bo referred to the fact that he loved to hunt. Hunt what—that was the question.

Dinner was in the main room, which was cozy and quaint. There was dim lighting and numerous photographs of famous people, some autographed. The tables were laid with white cloths, and each simple chair had a little seat cushion. There was always Italian music or something by Dean Martin or Frank Sinatra playing in the background. The meal usually started with clams oreganata, and for me, Joey saw that they arrived chopped. Joey started with a carafe of wine, and it was usually on the house. His main dish was always something meaty, like steak or veal Marsala or scaloppini. I usually asked for ravioli or shrimp. We rarely had dessert but always had black coffee with anisette. Joey joked that it would put hair on my chest.

I used to think he wished I had been a boy. In fact, he talked to me about traditionally male things: motorcycles, cars, his *paesanos* at the bar, bar fights, chess, novels like *The Hobbit*, airplanes, geography, history, war, politics, hunting, and weightlifting. His favorite people to talk to me about included Arnold Schwarzenegger, George Carlin, Robert DeNiro, Jimi Hendrix, Superman, Spiderman, "The Fonz," Eric Clapton, The Beatles, Merle Haggard, Johnny Cash, and Willie Nelson. He read a lot and seemed comfortable with these subjects, as opposed to things that would interest a little girl.

Some of this was boring to me at the time, but I tried to listen carefully and absorb everything Joey said. I craved any time he gave me, and if that meant listening to him about subjects I didn't really care about, then so be it. Little did I know that most of what he talked about would come in handy when I got older and started dating.

CHAPTER 5

JOEY ESPECIALLY LOVED TO TALK about airplanes and his job. It was his passion. When Joey took me to the airport, I always felt like someone important—or at least that I was *with* someone important. He was, after all, the leader of his union chapter.

I had never been on an airplane, so just being at the airport and seeing all the types of aircraft gave me a thrill. The biggest thrill came one day when Joey took me to the New York Tracon in Long Island. Tracon was an acronym for terminal radar approach control. That center was where a hundred or so controllers worked in a small, darkened room in front of radar screens. The screens showed dots that represented individual planes. Joey told me that the controllers were in charge of those dots.

Just hearing that made me nervous. They controlled the movement of all large aircraft in and out of the major metropolitan airports and others in Long Island, New Jersey, Westchester County, and upstate New York. The controllers at the Tracon guided the planes once they took off and then eventually handed them off to other major centers. Joey said they handled thousands of planes each day. He called it the busiest air traffic control center in the world. It sure looked that way to me.

In 1978, Joey hinted that he began feeling the turbulent tides within PATCO, the air traffic controllers union, the Professional Air Traffic Controller Organization, founded in 1967. Later as I got older, Joey explained the history of this union and his very important role. He told me that its goal was to maintain a national organization that represented the federal government's air traffic controllers. You see, in 1962 President Kennedy issued an order permitting federal employees to be represented by organizations that allowed for collective bargaining—basically, unions.

Joey was one of PATCO's chapter leaders, and in 1978 there were rumblings that a strike was on the way. I remember Joey was always flying to different cities for meetings. I didn't know the bigger picture when I was eight years old, I was just thrilled that he always brought me a snow globe from whatever city he had visited.

Even though he had a rough exterior and was cavalier at times, Joey was extremely intelligent, and he took his work seriously. You would think he'd be the first to start a picket line and strike, but surprisingly I found out that was not the case. Quite the contrary; he made it known he was against strike action. His advice was not to strike unless everyone could be on the same page. The controllers had a good gripe; they wanted better pay and pension plans, better hours, and better equipment. Who could blame them? These guys were locked up in these small, dark rooms, sometimes two shifts in a row, staring at tiny dots on a screen, which happened to represent hundreds of lives each. Talk about nerve-wracking. No wonder Joey drank a lot.

"I don't know what to do, Caroline," Joey said to my mother one day. "I need your advice, hon."

"This is getting to be a big deal, I guess," she said.

Joey was getting ready to fly to Las Vegas for a big meeting. He was over at our apartment, and I could feel his trepidation. We all could. It was one of the rare times he came to my mother for advice and was actually listening. He was sitting at the kitchen table putting out his cigarette in the ashtray. It was like something was happening that was bigger than any of us, and it wasn't going to be good.

"I mean we're all ready to do somethin', but we have to get our fuckin' issues straight and have every-fuckin'-body's participation. The conditions have to be right." Joey ran his fingers through his hair. He lit another cigarette, took a drag, and then slammed his fist on the table.

"I don't understand what the fuck is going on. The union was always so damn successful in gettin' things done and hearin' us guys, you know what I mean? It's like everyone is gangin' up to squash us."

"The big airlines are afraid of PATCO's power, and so is the government," Mom agreed.

"I just don't wanna back down," Joey said, frustrated. "I don't wanna take this shit they're givin' us. But striking could be a disaster too. My fuckin' job could be on the line. Not only that, gettin' this thing done is *everyone's* concern. No one wants a tragedy on our hands."

It was later written in a formal document that Joey cautioned those in charge at that meeting in Las Vegas "not to call a job action, because conditions didn't warrant it."

Joey said he felt the loudest voices for the strike were those from smaller hubs who didn't have good leadership. Realistically, if anyone were going to care, it would have to be the big boys representing the biggest cities. PATCO's president didn't take anyone's advice, and there was a slowdown.

Ultimately, Joey was right, and the bigmouths failed to deliver, leaving New York to come to their aid. It was the beginning of the end for Joey and many of the others. The slowdown had limited success, but what really hurt was that the powers-that-be started to see PATCO's lack of organizational support. After all was said and done, those groups who were against action to strike petitioned PATCO's leader to change procedures and implement a better system of checks and balances. This group was referred to as "Big 9, Crazy 8, and Little 7." This committee recognized the failure of the 1978 slowdown and took on the responsibility to educate PATCO and the air traffic controllers on what trade unionism was all about.

During the same period, Boston University School of Medicine was doing a health study on the occupation of air traffic controller. The results were published in a report to the Federal Aviation Administration (FAA). Joey made everyone read it, even me. He said it later backed up controllers' claims that there was a high burn-out factor to this job, which led to early retirement and second career training.

I remember Joey fuming about how the FAA downplayed the controllers' claims. He was sitting at the table at Grandpa Nunzio's house one Sunday morning while I was helping Nonna in the kitchen. Joey started getting into it, smoking a cigarette while Grandpa drank.

"These son of a bitches either have no fuckin' conception of what really goes on or they're just assholes," Joey shouted. "This is clearly unfair fuckin' labor practices. I mean, one of my fuckin' guys had a goddamned heart attack last week, and another fuckin' guy had a nervous breakdown last month. Most of these guys are like fuckin' ticking time bombs, and nobody gives a shit. These mothafuckas."

"Calm down, son," Grandpa Nunzio said. "What is PATCO requesting?"

"It's in the newspaper today," Joey answered. "You didn't see it?"

"No, I only got through the first two sections of the *Times* this morning."

"Well, it's in there. It's a little fuckin' blurb, no wonder you didn't fuckin' see it. This has been on the books, it's nothing new. The guys want the fuckin' cost of living increase, better pay, shorter workweek, and safety enhancements. It's only right. I mean, what the fuck? Throw us a bone.

"And then this study is out that backs us up, and they want to brush it under the carpet. It's like we're not even being heard. Too bad it's not the mafia. They take care of their fuckin' people who do right by them. Those guys could really teach the FAA a couple of things."

After that, Joey was on a mission. He became a spokesperson for PATCO. He had speaking engagements at colleges and high schools. He even spoke at my elementary school. He didn't just come to career day in my class; he spoke to the entire school and faculty in the auditorium. I was so proud of him with his charts and graphs, speaking in front of the whole school. Even if the material was a little over our heads and it seemed as though he had an axe to grind, it was still impressive to me. All my little friends were more impressed with the fact that he looked like a badass and had big biceps. I've got to admit, it made me feel cool.

So the fact that I idolized him for a time didn't help in the times he disappointed me. It only made the blow even more crushing. One example was during football season. He used to like to do two things at once, like watching football and reading the *TV Guide* or doing a crossword puzzle. He said it relaxed him. I used to get so excited when he was visiting at our apartment that I would run up to snuggle behind him on the couch. Sometimes I would throw my arms around him, but I could tell this annoyed him if the game was on. He would shoo me away and tell me to go sit somewhere else.

However, the biggest blows came the times I would wait by the window for him to come get me on his days to visit—and he didn't show up.

One of those times I was sitting on the window sill, playing with my dolls, casting glances for him out the window.

"Just look at her!" Crazy Nana said. "She has no idea he's two hours late. She looks pathetic."

"I know but what would you like me to do about it? I can't get in touch with him," Mom said, gritting her teeth together.

"He's nothing but a punk hood," Nana growled. "If I had him in front of me, I'd smash his face right into the wall. He'll get his one day. I'll fix him."

She was always going to "fix" someone, as if they were broken. And how exactly was she going to "fix" him? Did she have some superhuman power? Did she know witchcraft? Maybe she was the head witch. Whatever the case, she didn't like anyone messing with her children or grandchildren. She was a protective matriarch.

All of a sudden, the phone rang. My mother answered it.

"Where the hell are you? Yeah … oh really … Well then, you tell her! Nina, come to phone," she started calmly. "It's your father!" She was screaming by the time she reached last syllable.

"Hello, Dad, are you on your way?"

"No, hon, not today," Joey answered. "I got tied up. I'm sorry. You know I love ya, right?"

"Yup."

"I'll make it up to ya," he said. "You're a good kid, don't give your mother any trouble."

Joey chuckled, but I just bit my lip to hold back the tears.

Every time he did this to me I was always so disappointed. He would always end the conversation with "I love ya, you know."

I would always answer, "I know," but I really didn't know.

On days when he would come get me, he was always late, but I was thrilled to see him anyway.

For quite some time, Joey seemed even more preoccupied than ever when we were together. He was always flying to different conferences, and his visits with me were few and far between. Not only that, he was still working crazy hours and was still on a mission to have PATCO's voice heard.

PATCO was an organization that stood up for what it believed, and Joey was becoming one of its loudest choir-boys. The FAA was insulting at times and tried everything to curb PATCO's power.

Meanwhile, PATCO had very little success at convincing President Jimmy Carter's administration to have the FAA ease up. That was one reason why PATCO endorsed Ronald Reagan for President of the United States.

In 1980, the new PATCO president met with Ronald Reagan, who assured everyone of his support for the controllers. In fact, on October 20, 1980, Reagan committed this to writing. Three days later, PATCO publicly endorsed Reagan. As promised, negotiations finally took place in 1981; however, key members of the Department of Transportation failed to show up, and soon the writing was on the wall. The men and women of PATCO had been duped.

"They got to Reagan," Joey said to Grandpa. "They fuckin' got to him. That fuckin' actor."

On this particular Sunday morning I could tell everyone was tense. Joey hadn't been sleeping well and seemed very depressed. At times he was just looking down and fiddling with his cigarette pack. He lit one right after the other.

Nonna kept telling him, "Well, what ya gonna do? You can't fight the system."

I sat silently, looking at a magazine, pretending I wasn't listening to their conversation.

Grandpa was a staunch Republican and thought it was futile to keep fighting.

"I know you're disappointed, and it's unfortunate it has to be this way, but think of how much better things will be on the whole with a Republican in office. The hostages are back, and the economy is picking up."

"Yeah, I know, Dad, good for everyone else, and fuck you!" Joey said matter-of-factly. "Where's your fuckin' loyalty? And how small-minded are you that you don't fuckin' think this is gonna affect anyone else? How about other unions? How 'bout if we do strike, and we probably will, how will this affect the economy and the country?"

On one hand, Joey sort of got what he wished for—an administration with a mob mentality—but it backfired. And now Joey was fired up.

"Let me explain something to you, Pop," he said, taking command of the kitchen. "The FAA was successful in getting the Reagan Administration to see that if you get rid of PATCO, you get rid of a problem. He broke his fuckin' written promise to this union and will to many others—you'll see. What a slap in the face."

Joey looked into the glass ashtray that had "Caesar's Palace" inscribed on it in gold. He chuckled, and commented that he had bought it for Grandpa at his last work trip to Vegas. Now, I could only guess he was contemplating his future and his next move.

President Reagan was indeed known to have an anti-union philosophy. So in the summer of 1981, with contracts expired and no one listening to their pleas, PATCO led a strike.

"Listen, Caroline, don't worry," Joey said. "Believe me, none of us wanted this. But my back is up against the wall with this clown in office. We gotta take a stand. This time we're more prepared."

"So what are your options, now?" my mother asked. "I mean, you could lose your job because of this. We're struggling as it is."

Mom was always the worrier. Joey was never great about providing cash to support her. She worked as a secretary but as a single mother, also trying to provide for Nana, finances were always on her mind.

"Jeez, Caroline, you and Nina will be fine," he said. "You gotta look at the bigger picture. Anyway, we have a plan to go back to work immediately if talks are attempted. If not, we'll be on strike. What the fuck else can I say? Let's get real here, okay. I'm scared. I don't know what else to do. We've been down this road before, you and me, and you gave me good advice last time. Last time it was easier not to do this thing. Now I've kinda got no choice."

There was a long pause.

"Are you okay, Joey?"

"Do you know I've never been afraid of anything, really until now." His voice broke. "Are you on my side or what?"

"I am," she answered. "Good luck. And Joey—be careful."

My mother was always there for Joey if he needed her, no matter what their relationship was like. But she was never quite confident that he would be there for her. In any case, she said she really did hope PATCO's plan would work and the strike would succeed.

However, that same day, President Reagan had a very different plan. It was his "Rose Garden Ultimatum." In a nutshell, the message was, "get back to work or be terminated." Union members went crazy, taking to the streets, parks, parking lots, and camping out in tents. They banded together against injustice.

It's times like these when groups are clearly divided into followers and leaders. Joey was definitely a leader, partly because he would never back down from a challenge. While some hung their heads in their hands, Joey went charging full force. He saw red. Whatever trepidation he had before disappeared. His ego soared, and there was no stopping him.

"Caroline, you watching the fuckin' news?" Joey was in hysterics.

"Yeah, I heard it in the background," Mom answered.

She usually never watched the news but said it was relevant these days. "I'm trying to get dinner on. What's so funny? I don't find any of this funny."

"Good ol' Merle!" he shouted. "The guys in Tampa were on the fuckin' news singing 'Take this Job and Shove It!' I bet ya fuckin' Merle Haggard is waving his cowboy hat proudly. We're making fuckin' history. This is classic."

"By the way, Caroline, check me out on the eleven o'clock," Joey announced. "I'm going down for an interview to speak out against this mothafucka and our rights as air traffic controllers and Americans."

"Oh boy, you're on a roll," Mom joked. "I better get out of your way. In all seriousness, just please watch it a little. You have a daughter to think of. Don't get crazy."

"Yeah, calm down, calm down. I got it under control."

The interview went well. I remember my mother let me stay up past my bedtime to watch it. She said he couldn't curse on television, so how bad could it be? Besides, it wasn't every day you got to see your parent on TV.

Joey looked a little anxious, but dapper in a suit. The reporter fired away questions at Joey, who sat on the couch beside him. He answered every one without hesitation, forcefully and to the point. He never even cracked a smile. Even though he had an invincible attitude, this interview would soon be the nail in his coffin. Sure enough, with a direct order from Reagan, Joey was fired, just like that.

Some say it was this strike that hardened the government's anti-union position. Nevertheless, the gavel was coming down hard. While some controllers were scared into going back to work, madness broke out. Sixty-four arrest warrants were issued, and the FBI got involved. Allegedly, anti-union supporters made phone threats and made secret visits with guns. Harassment was rampant throughout the country.

"That son of a bitch, bastard fired me," Joey shouted over the phone to Caroline.

"That's it hon, I'm done."

"No, you're not!" she answered. "Don't talk like that. You're better than that. You're smart, for God's sake. You could do anything."

"I know, we were all smart, Caroline."

Indeed, all the controllers were smart and accomplished. According to the health study in 1978, of the 416 men and women in the northeast, 99 percent served between two and twenty-two years in the armed services. Some were high ranking, and some were even pilots for the military. Joey knew all this information about the men and women he worked with. Heck, he probably knew some of them better than he knew Mom and me.

"I can't do a goddamned thing about it," Joey lamented. "What's worse, I don't think getting another job is going to be easy. They got an anti-PATCO/union public relations campaign going on. It's like a witch hunt."

"Oh, you're exaggerating," my mom said.

"No fuckin' way," Joey said indignantly. "You don't watch the news or read the paper, but it's out there. The government is portraying a striker as a greedy and disloyal American. They're tricking the fuckin' public and focusing on some bullshit oath that federal employees take not to strike. That shit was declared unconstitutional, but the layperson wouldn't know that."

"Really?"

"Yeah, really!" He was all fired up. "If that wasn't bad enough, the strike is causing turmoil for lots of industries."

Mail, airline, and travel were among those affected by the chaos.

"We're the negative poster child for unions now, which is gonna make it a whole hell of a lot easier for this rat bastard to restructure things the way he wants them. That's it. I'm through."

And he was, at least in that industry. Then, as time went on, he said he realized that he was through in other industries as well. And so were his cohorts. Many social services, except food stamps, were cut off for those who had participated in the strike. Certain corporations were advised not to hire a striker. PATCO no longer existed, although many of the die-hards would disagree, saying it had just been reorganized. Nevertheless, many lives were ruined.

Joey became depressed and went on drinking sprees till all hours of the night. He lost his apartment after it went co-op and stayed with Grandpa Nunzio for a while. After raising hell and causing a couple of arguments that left holes in Grandpa's wall, he eventually moved in with his girlfriend, Patti, because he had no place to live. It didn't seem he would ever get his act together. He kept having delusions that the powers that be were working on getting the old contollers' jobs back. He scoured the newspaper every day in search of any tidbit on the situation. He drank tons of coffee and smoked even more. He lifted weights obsessively in Patti's basement, but after a while, he lost his passion for that too.

CHAPTER 6

IN THE MEANTIME, MOM MET Harry. They met at a work function, and he said she was the most gorgeous green-eyed beauty he had ever seen. For him, it was love at first sight. Both he and my mother say they felt as though they had known each other forever. They started dating without my knowledge. My mom was careful not to bring guys home unless she was serious.

Besides that, the last guy she brought home made me queasy. He was tall and wore a toupee. It looked like a piece of carpet to me. When he came to the house to pick her up for a date, this toupee guy always wore a suit, as though he was going to work or somewhere important. He always came with gifts for me, but I could see right through that move. You can't buy someone's affection. Hell, I knew that and I was only a kid. I would just roll my eyes at her when I knew she had a date with him—but not with Harry.

When I finally met Harry, I was a little hesitant to welcome him, but he was funny and a straight shooter. A Jewish, unthreatening-looking guy from Queens, Harry always made me feel safe, like he could take care of any situation. And his family was a dream. I had hit the welcome wagon jackpot! Harry had two brothers with down-to-earth wives and kids. These people couldn't have been nicer. I had two, new, ready-made families with kids my age. In addition, Harry's father was the cutest old man I had ever seen, and very loving to me. I had to pinch myself. To top it all off, Harry had two boys, my age, from a previous marriage. I was going to have stepbrothers. Wowee! Needless to say, I was really pulling for Harry.

But then there was Crazy Nana…. She hated Joey and certainly didn't like Harry at first, nor anyone else who tried to get close to my mother. But Harry was so kind and so confident in himself that he wasn't going to let Nana stand in his way.

"Ohhh, he's coming here again," Nana half-whispered to me in the kitchen as the doorbell rang. "You gotta be shittin' me. Your mother didn't tell me that."

"Yes she did, Nana, don't you remember?"

"Must've forgot." She shrugged. "Quiet, he just walked in."

"So?"

"I want to hear what their plans are, child!" Nana answered me impatiently.

"Why don't you just ask them?"

Nana just eavesdropped by the hallway.

"Fine, I'll go ask them," I said.

I breezed by Nana into the living room and gave Harry a big bear hug. Mom excused herself to the bathroom.

"Hey, Nina!" Harry exclaimed. "How are you, sweetheart?"

It felt wonderful that he was always so happy to see me.

"Great! And what are you and Mom up to today?"

"Hmm," Nana muttered as she entered the room.

"Oh hello, Rose!" Harry said with exaggeration. "How are you today?"

"Yeah, good, and you?"

"Never better," he answered.

Nana wanted to cut through the small talk. She simply wanted to know how the days plans were going to affect her. She always acted busy, but she rarely had anything going on. Her priorities consisted of going to the Laundromat, getting her hair done, watching her soap operas, visiting her sisters, and shopping with my mother. Anything other than that was not important to her.

"Well, answer the poor girl," Nana complained. "She just asked you for the game plan."

"For what … football?" He had fun antagonizing Nana, and she secretly liked it too.

"Oh, go on, Harry! You know what I mean—for today. Nobody tells me anything around here."

"Oh, you are so neglected," my mother said sarcastically as she came into the room.

"Never mind you," Nana retorted. "How is a person supposed to know what to wear or when to get ready? Last night you should have told me what you were going to be doing today. It is Saturday, after all. I thought we were going shopping."

Nana liked to know everything. She was also a creature of habit.

"Well, don't you just wake up early and get ready for the day like most people your age, Rose?" Harry asked. "My father is up at the crack of dawn, making breakfast, taking out the trash, and reading the paper."

"Good for him," she answered childishly. "And what do you mean by *most people my age?* I'll have you know that when Caroline and I are out together, people think I am her sister, my dear boy."

"Oh yeah, I could see that," Harry joked.

My mother interrupted to tell Nana and me that she and Harry would be dropping us off in the Bronx on their way to the City to see a play. They would pick us up on their way back home a couple of hours later.

Nana and I were to spend the day with her two sisters. I called them the "crooner cronies" because they were always either talking or singing. The three of them loved to get together and harmonize. No matter what they were doing, when they broke into song, they'd just keep on going. One might be applying lipstick; the other wiping the table, while the other was dancing a jig. It was typical. The only time they stayed somewhat quiet was to eat. The crooner cronies were a hoot, and I always got an education when I spent time with them. They were Irish-Americans, and they were all a little rough around the edges.

Ruthie was the oldest sister and the most crass. They all told it like it was, but she cursed worse than a sailor. While she was busy raising a family, she waited tables nights and some early-morning shifts, so she had some rough customers. She was a tough woman, a little masculine, with a voice husky from smoking. She took no bullshit from anyone, especially kids, so I was always on my best behavior at her house.

She lived in a walk-up apartment on a block where you could always join some kind of ballgame in the street, any time of day. Kids were always outside playing. Cars didn't seem to have the right of way back then. And God forbid anyone drove through her street fast and disturbed the neighborhood kids playing. They would grab whatever they had in their hand, whether a ball or a rock, and throw it at the car speeding by.

Ruthie's husband, Artie, was usually hanging around the house, but I never really got to know anything about him—maybe because he could never get a word past the crooner cronies.

Rona was the middle sister, and she was wild. Also a waitress, she married and had kids, but after her husband died she had many suitors. It seemed as if her home had a revolving door, but she was the one calling the shots. If something about the man didn't suit her—for instance, if he didn't bring her flowers or candy—she dismissed him.

My nana, Rose, was the baby. She was the beauty of the bunch, with a svelte body and alluring green eyes. She told the story that as children, the older two were always trying to protect her from a very violent father. So when the day came that she could get away from the house by doing the one thing she loved more than anything else in the world, that's exactly what she did....

CHAPTER 7

It was her passion for dancing that saved Rose from her miserable home life. She had talent, and in the late 1930s she danced all over the City. She traveled with vaudeville and some other shows before she was even eighteen. She often lied to producers about her age or had friends sign consent forms to allow her to go on different gigs.

She rubbed elbows with a number of young actors on their way to making it big. One of her friends, Harriet, actually changed her name to something cute and catchy, on the advice of a Hollywood producer, to make her more marketable. Harriet and Rose were always neck and neck for parts at auditions. Often, they traveled and performed together, and they became friends and rivals. Many times my nana, Rose, told me and others the circumstances that changed their friendship. I remember the story of these two women as a life lesson.

One day an agent who was part of a big song-and-dance production being filmed in Hollywood came to New York City to find raw talent. He spotted Harriet and Rose.

"Oh my Gawd, how do I look, Rose?" Harriet asked.

"Don't be so full of yourself. How do *I* look?" Rose wondered.

"Listen, we both look great, that's not the problem," Harriet said. "We better dance our hearts out for this guy. That's what he really wants to see."

So in a line of many showgirls on stage, one by one, each dancer performed when called upon while the others stood there. Then each woman would get called up to the front of the stage for a question-and-answer session. Again, Rose was asked about her age, and again she had to lie. She did so gladly, knowing that this show would be her ticket to fame and fortune, far away from life as she knew it. She wanted it so badly.

Both she and Harriet, among some others, were eventually selected that day for the show.

"I'm so excited, I have to pinch myself!" Rose exclaimed. "Could this really be true?"

"I know, Rose," Harriet said. "This is quite extraordinary. Two good friends from the same neighborhood making it this far together—it's incredible!"

That would have been a great sentiment if she had meant it. Unfortunately, Harriet had other plans. She had some experience in California already, and she knew how things worked. She also knew her time to become a somebody out there was limited. Now she would be traveling to Hollywood with Rose, a younger, prettier, more adept dancer. However, Harriet knew Rose's secret.

"Rose, would you be a dear and keep an eye on my things?" Harriet asked.

"Certainly, take your time," Rose answered. She was on cloud nine. All she could think about was her big break. But time passed, and Rose grew concerned about what could be taking Harriet so long. She glanced behind the stage curtain, down the long corridor, and spotted Harriet speaking with a gentleman. She waited a little longer.

Harriet snuck up behind Rose. "I'm back," she said. "I'm so sorry I took so long, but I had to use the lavatory."

"Who were you speaking with back there?"

"Oh, he was just a stage manager," Harriet said. "I was asking him about choreography."

Just then, Rose got called backstage. A man with horn-rimmed glasses and a fedora looked sternly at her and asked her to tell him her age.

"Miss, you had better think hard about how you answer this question," he said. "We don't look kindly upon those who stretch the truth."

There was silence.

"Are you eighteen yet?" he asked.

There was even more silence.

"Look here, missy, tell me the truth," the man demanded. "I'm the producer of this show. How 'bout I put your mind at ease? If you are not eighteen yet, just have your father come down here tomorrow and sign for you."

Rose knew her father would never do this—and so did Harriet. At that point, she knew she had been betrayed. Harriet was to blame. Rose was about to confront her, but when she pulled back the stage curtain, Harriet was gone. Most of the dancers had left.

"Where is everyone?" Rose asked the few women who remained.

"They told us to go home," one of the dancers said. "They want us to get a good night sleep before we leave on the bus tomorrow."

Rose couldn't believe Harriet had left without her; they were a team. But now she knew that had changed. She also knew this was going to be a long night. She would have to go home and ask her father to sign a consent form.

When Rose finally reached her house, she was tired and hungry, but all she cared about was getting her dad to do this one thing for her.

"Have you lost your mind, child?" her father shouted. "I am not signing any damn paper. That is your ticket to self-destruction."

"But please, please," Rose pleaded. "This would be so great for me. I could live my dream and get discovered."

"The only dream you better have is in your bed, while you're sleeping," he said. "You're just a girl. Do you know what they do to pretty young things out there? They chew them up and spit them out. Besides, I am your father, and I'm responsible for you. Case closed. Now get in your old room before I have to get my belt out. I'm sure you remember my belt. I can refresh your memory if need be. This is reality, girl. Better wake up from your silly fantasy!"

These words stung worse than any belt could have. Rose cried her eyes out that night. Her father could hear her sobbing, which made him even angrier. Every time he passed by her door, he slammed it with his fist and warned her to quiet down. She finally stuffed her face into her pillow and tried to come up with a plan. Exhausted, she finally fell asleep.

Rose woke up with the sun and splashed some water on her face. Her eyes were almost swollen shut. She grabbed her things and headed off to the rehearsal hall in hopes of a miracle. When she arrived, she saw some of the girls she had auditioned with boarding a big bus. Just then Harriet started climbing on, and she called out to her.

"Why did you do this to me!" Rose shouted.

Visibly startled, Harriet stared at Rose vacantly and then looked away.

Crushed, Rose mumbled under her breath, "I hope you will never be happy again, you pathetic, wretched girl."

Rose was frozen still. She just stood there and punished herself by watching every last one of the dancers get on the bus. When she spotted the producer, she ran up to him in desperation. With tears running down her face, she pleaded with him to make an exception.

"Please, mister, let me go along," Rose begged. "I'll clean rooms, I'll scrub toilets, whatever you need me to do, I'll gladly do it. I'm begging you for this chance."

"Look here, miss, rules are rules," the producer told her. "I'll tell you what, next year I will be back scouting for talent again. You'll be old enough, and if you're just as good, then you'll be a shoe-in. Rose could only look away for fear she would start bawling. In her mind there was no next year; it was now or never.

"For what it's worth, you are a very good dancer. Keep your chin up. kid."

That was it. He walked away and got on the bus. Rose stood at the corner and watched as the bus pulled out of sight. The rejection was too much for her. Her head was spinning, and she could hardly swallow. As she turned to walk away, tears ran down her motionless face. She was numb. It was the kind of crying that comes when you're dead inside but the tears won't stop. She cried like that all the way to Ruthie's house. She knew Ruthie would take her in.

Rose eventually got a job at a movie theater ticket booth. She performed in some small shows and slept at her sisters' houses most of the time to avoid her father. Her disdain for him deepened now that he had disappointed her so deeply. She felt he had owed it to her to do this one thing for her after the miserable life he had shown her. Once he made it clear he wouldn't do it, she wanted nothing more to do with him.

A couple of months later, she met an extremely intelligent Italian man named John who was much older than her. He was successful, tall, and thin and had gentle, puppy dog eyes. He was enamored and seemed to think she had a funny way about her. First he came to see Rose at the ticket booth on a weekly basis. Weekly turned into nightly. The months went by, and soon he asked for her hand in marriage. He told Rose he didn't care about her age, that he was deeply in love with her. Rose jumped at the chance for marriage. She figured that even though this wasn't her dream, it was a way out of her neighborhood and a chance at having her own life.

They married and had children immediately. When the first one, Mario, came, motherhood threw Rose for a loop. She could barely take care of herself, and now she had a husband and a child as well. She was always nervous, a worrier. She tried to put off having more children, but eventually two more came, back to back, Caroline and Vinny, sending her into a tailspin.

When she eventually had a nervous breakdown, her sisters were there to pick up the pieces. Rona and Ruthie helped take care of the kids for a short time until Rose was better. She suffered from anxiety and started having delusions, believing she had special powers and could put curses on people.

In the meantime, Harriet had made the big time out in Hollywood and was cast in a couple of movies. This made Rose furious, and she used to pace back and forth in her house cursing Harriet and the day she had laid eyes on her. Harriet had also married and had a child. The child was not well, and it was no secret that this took a toll on her and her career.

While Rose would rest in her room every afternoon, she listened to the radio. One day on the news, she learned that Harriet's husband had left her. Harriet was currently hospitalized and being treated for a mental breakdown.

"I knew it!" Rose shouted. "She's no better than me. That witch will never have a happy life for what she did to me. That's the way the world works. Believe you me!"

Then Rose had a revelation.

"Wait a minute," she mumbled. "Maybe I did this ... maybe my prayers for her to be miserable worked. I must be an *actual* witch."

She thought about it for a minute and then with a smug look said, "That'll teach ya to mess with me, ya bastard."

So that was it. She was a witch with special powers, and nobody had better mess with her. Rose told everyone this story and urged them all to keep it quiet, as if it were top-secret information. This is why I've come to know her as "Crazy Nana."

The irony is that even though Harriet's misery was public knowledge because she was in the spotlight, Nana also seemed miserable. She would never get over her missed opportunities. This was obvious. She would never use her talent for good or try to succeed with it in other ways. She wasted it, and it seemed to bother her forever, no mater what other good came along. Regret and fear consumed her thoughts and actions and got in the way of the kind of wife and mother she could've been. She was a prisoner of her own mind. Her life was not miserable by anyone's standards but her own. She was married to a man who loved her dearly, and they had three healthy, beautiful children. That is success enough for many people. She knew it but never truly appreciated it, and never knew true happiness.

CHAPTER 8

THAT DAY WITH THE CROONER cronies was uneventful, but any time I spent with all of them was an education. I learned how to wipe down a table *the right way* from Ruthie, how to put on red lipstick from Rona, and how to fold clothes—and of course dance—from Nana. They continually argued about how the other ones did each task.

"You have too much soap on the sponge," Rona snipped at Ruthie.

"Never you mind woman," Ruthie retorted. "You could lick the table when I am done with it. I can assure you that's how clean it will be. Better pay attention to your lips before you wind up looking like a clown."

"Oh please, I could do this with my eyes closed," Rona answered. "You just wish you knew *how* to put on makeup. You should pay attention to Rose. She's not folding those towels right."

"Oh Rona you are always looking to start trouble." Rose said. And around and around they would go with their comical criticisms.

They smoked so many cigarettes and talked about so many people that I wondered when they would give their mouths a break. By the end of my day with them, I was the one who needed a break. While they got into a pow-wow about one of their relatives, I snuck away to the couch to sit with Artie and watch some television until Harry and Mom came to pick us up.

My mother and Harry always seemed to get along fabulously; even the car ride back home was pleasant, no stress. And that's how things remained for a while.

By the time I got to middle school and reached my teen years,

Joey's visits were scarce. I was angry that he didn't take more of an interest in me. I think having Harry in my life made the differences in parenting very apparent to me. But I accepted Joey's unusual ways and sometimes I felt sad for him. I went to a Catholic middle school where the nuns were very strict. I considered myself a good girl, and I mostly stayed out of trouble. However, these ladies meant business and frowned upon any transgression. For minor infractions I had my ears pulled and rulers slammed on my hands. None of it really hurt; it was more embarrassing than anything else.

Now, if you're thinking my mother went to the school and gave the nuns hell for any of this, think again. Back in those days, if you got into trouble at school, your parents received a phone call, and you'd better pray for mercy when you got home. That's just the way it was. Parents sided with the teachers, and the "tough love" at home got results, that's for sure.

Now, because I was a good student overall, I rarely got called to the principal's office. So when I did get a call, I was perplexed. Was I in trouble? Had I forgotten something at home? Maybe I was getting an award for something…. Nah, I hadn't done anything outstanding. What could it be? All I knew was that the nun escorting me looked concerned. When I stepped into the principal's office, everyone there looked concerned.

"Okay, sit down dear," the principal said nervously.

Now I was worried. I just hoped nobody I knew was dead.

"We've spoken to your nana," he said. "She told us your mother is away on a short vacation, so your nana will be coming to pick you up. Sweetheart, it seems your father is in the hospital. He tried to commit suicide last night."

I just looked at all of them as they stared at me. I didn't know what to say. I certainly knew what suicide was, but I had never known anybody who actually attempted it.

"Are you okay, sweetheart?" he asked. "Do you understand what I'm telling you?"

I nodded. Of course I understood. Was he an idiot? What was I supposed to do? Did they want me to burst into tears or start vomiting? I had so many questions that I knew these jokers wouldn't be able to answer, so I just kept quiet. They all left me alone, and I couldn't wait for Nana to get there. I knew she would have the answers.

While I waited, I saw a comforting face approaching from down the hallway. It was Father O'Malley, a priest at the school and church. He was a good man, patient and understanding and not old and stuffy, as some priests were. He had salt-and-pepper colored hair and gentle blue eyes. His homilies were strong and relevant. I would only go to confession when I knew he was conducting it. He had helped me out many times when I was confused or sad about Joey and mom's relationship splitting apart. He knew my history and was always willing to lend an ear. He was everything I thought a priest should be, and I looked up to him, like an uncle or a grandpa.

"Hello, Nina. I heard the news," he said, reaching out his hand. "How are you taking it?"

"I'm okay," I answered as I put my hand in his. "I'm glad to see you."

"Oh, I came right over for you. Listen, I know sometimes adults find themselves in precarious situations and react in ways that are confusing to others, especially young adults."

I loved that he never referred to people my age as "kids" or "children." He was very respectful, and this was before it was politically correct.

"Is it stuffy in here?" he asked. "Let's take a walk."

When we exited the room, he told me he just wanted to get me out of the office to avoid any busybodies. I was grateful.

"You've certainly had to grow up early, Nina. It's not such a bad thing, you know. Your dad will be fine, and you'll find that you gain a lot of wisdom from all of this. You can't see it now, but everything happens for a reason that only God knows. He has a plan for all of us. What are your thoughts?"

"I don't know yet," I said. "I guess my father is just very depressed. I wish I could understand him and help. I wish I could know him."

"You don't feel like you know him as a person, or as a father?"

I paused. Then the question hit me, and I answered, "Neither."

He was a little taken aback. Then he stopped and stared at me.

"You know none of this has anything to do with you, right?" he said.

I nodded in agreement.

"You're going to be fine, my dear."

CHAPTER 9

Fifteen Years Later - JOEY

I GUESS YOU REALLY NEVER know how you're going to react when a doc tells you that you have cancer. There I was just walking down the street like I always did—granted, a lot slower than I used to—but now I knew for sure I was sick, terminally. I could walk right past the people I always did, and nothing would be different to them. Meanwhile, everything was different to me. My days were numbered, as were most people's. The only difference for me was that I knew my number: 180 at best. Six months! Isn't that some shit? And then I saw a stray dog peeing in the snow by a fire hydrant; how appropriate.

"How ya doin' buddy? You don't mind if I sit here on this bench while ya do your business?" I asked rhetorically.

After a couple of slow, enjoyable drags on my cigarette, I just had to laugh out loud. If I didn't, I thought I would crack inside. Don't get me wrong, I knew I was sick. I had a bunch of ailments starting to take hold of me, but I either tried to beat them or learned to live with them. I never really considered anything being fatal. After all, I was invincible. Or so I thought. I had cheated death so many times before: motorcycle accidents, bar fights, overdoses, you name it. Came through like a champ every time ... every fuckin' time. I came through even when I didn't want to.

Not only that, but my whole life, it seemed, was a counterbalance of excesses. Maybe I thought that would buy me a few years. I mean, I had smoked, drank, and done drugs since I could remember; but I also worked out and took vitamins, supplements, not to mention a little HGH and steroids. For Christ's sake, I had the physique of a bodybuilder. I still had the python biceps. Ah, what ya gonna do. It is what it is.

As I hobbled up on my good leg and balanced with my cane to make the rest of the journey home, I started thinking about one person: Nina. How was I gonna tell her this? We had just started talking again after so much lost time. I finally had my chance to get connected, even if it was long-distance. Do right for all my wrongs. Now that chance was gone. There was the irony in life.

My apartment in the Bronx was old, dusty, and cluttered with books—just the way I liked it. It was a one-room efficiency with creaking, wooden floors and scuffed walls that had turned a dingy beige from cigarette smoke. It was all I can afford with social security and government assistance. I couldn't handle too much responsibility anyway, or so I'd been told.

On the other hand, I deserved a lot better than this at the end of my life. I was at the top of my game as an air traffic controller and had more responsibility with that job than most do in a lifetime. People's lives were in the palms of my hands, literally. I should be collecting handsomely right now, but that was shot to shit after the strike. I got tossed in the garbage. My own government turned its back on me, and I was in the military, for God's sake. I deserved a lot better than what I got. What ya gonna do.

In my apartment, the white phone was like an elephant in the room, just staring at me, waiting for me to make a move. I should call my daughter and tell her the news. And why didn't I? Probably for the same reason that kept me from calling her all these years. Fear. Fear of how to react if Nina cried. I mean, what the fuck would I say? I was never good at comforting her. I guess by now she didn't need comforting. I suppose I just didn't want to cause her pain again. I dunno, maybe she wouldn't even care. I just thought things would be so different with us talking again and all. I thought my chance to make amends was here. Well, that was shot to shit, so what ya gonna do.

Maybe the phone was taunting me.… I wasn't gonna let it win, that was for sure. I mean, what did I have to lose at this point? *Well, here goes nothing*, I thought. I dialed.

"Hello, Nina. It's your father," I said.

"Wow, I didn't think you'd be calling again so soon," she said.

"This is a record five times since our first conversation on Christmas. Are you sure Aunt Joanne's not there making you call me?"

"Don't get cute."

She was like her mother in that respect. She always tried to turn something good I did into something bad. She acted like I had an ulterior motive. It used to send me over the edge when her mother got like that. Really burned me up inside. What, did they think I had no fuckin' feelings? I should've never told her Joanne was in the room with me Christmas Eve when I called. I knew she fuckin' thought I was forced into calling her. Truth be told, I was nervous. I just needed a little push, that was all. I wished to God this kid wasn't so proud and sarcastic all the time.

"How are you?" she asked. "Are you feeling okay?"

This was it. My chance to tell her, but I couldn't bring the words out. Just then I realized I hadn't told Charo. *I really need to tell her before anyone else. I'll tell Nina another time.*

"I'm good. Just got this nagging cough I can't shake," I said.

"Oh, because your voice sounds so weak. That cough must be a deep one."

"Ya know, it's still so friggin' cold up here. That never helps when you're sick. I got chronic bronchitis anyway. I'd love to be in sunny Florida with you guys. One day maybe."

"You know, Dad, It's nice that you're staying in touch with me," she said. "I'm really happy about it—sad that we've lost so much time, but glad we're making up for it. Some people never get another chance."

"I know, I know," I answered her hurriedly. She was making me misty and pissed at the same time. I mean, what she said was true, we had this chance, but little did she know how brief it would be. "I gotta go. I hear Charo coming in. I'll call ya in a couple days. I love ya."

So there it went. I didn't want to tell her yet. I just couldn't.

CHAPTER 10

"IT'S BEEN TWO WEEKS AND I'm doing okay, really," I told my sister, Joanne, over the phone. "You're worrying too much."

"No she isn't," yelled Charo in the background. "You betta tell her, Joey, babee. Don't leesten to him, Yoanna, he been throwin' up blood in the bowl, my dear."

Joanne's voice was full of concern. "Maybe you should put her on the phone, Joey, so I can get the real story—and I can tell her how to say my name right for the fiftieth time."

"Haa, don't make me laugh," I said, coughing.

And I kept coughing. *Oh great, now's not the time for it to get out of control.*

"You see, you're choking to death," Joanne exclaimed. "That's it, I'm coming down tomorrow and taking you to the doctor. I want to be there for the straight story."

"I'm sick, goddamnit!" I struggled to shout at her. "I told you, I have cancer. What the fuck else do you wanna know?"

"I want to know what the prognosis is, what the treatment is, if you're on the right medications, if you need something that Medicare won't cover, things like that."

"Don't you think I know those things already?" I asked. "Don't you think I know how to take care of myself?"

Couldn't she see how hard this was already? I mean, for Christ's sake, my manhood was being taken away slowly but surely as I wilted away to nothing, and now she wanted to take away my dignity by treating me like a fuckin' child.

"No!" she retorted. "You act like a real fucking asshole, you know.

I'm your sister, and I want to help you. You've always come to me for everything—money, favors—and I've always been there. Now I want to help you possibly get better, and you're pushing me away. Gee, I don't know, call me selfish, but I want to know firsthand what the doctor has to say. Is that okay?"

This bitch wasn't gonna let up. *My kid sister comes to the rescue as usual. I guess I'll entertain her. She's only setting herself up for disappointment, though.*

"Yeah, since you put it so nicely, I guess it's okay," I answered. "The appointment is at tree."

"You mean three."

"What are you, an English teacher all of a sudden?" I quipped. "Don't get cute, you know what I mean."

And that's how it went with us. We'd get loud with each other and then always joked. She tried to get tough with me, but it never worked. Although I did feel bad when I hurt her feelings. After our visit with the oncologist, I could tell she was rattled. I could also tell the wheels in her head were spinning.

"Listen, here's what we're gonna do, Joey," she started as we drove away. "My father in-law has a guy in the Bronx that he swears by. Says he saved his best friend's life. We're gonna get a second opinion."

"Stop, stop, stop!" I shouted. "I'm not a fuckin' science project, Joanne. The fuckin' doc told you I have stage four lung cancer and showed you the X-rays and the CT scan. What more do you need to see?"

"Maybe this guy knows about a treatment that your guy doesn't know about," she reasoned. "Joey, there are experimental drugs now that could help you. Maybe they could shrink the cancer or put it in remission. You know, talking to you is like talking to the wall. I'm going to look on the Internet. Are you even listening? What are you doing? Don't tell me you're going to light that in my car."

"A, oh, back off," I said playfully. "I got to have some pleasure left. You gonna tell me I can't have a smoke in your presence?"

"Not in my car," she said sassily. "I don't want your secondhand smoke or that smell. And you have some nerve smoking when you know you have lung cancer. Our father would be cursing you out right now if he were alive to see this."

"Good ol' Nunzio. Yeah, lucky bastard died of a heart attack. Didn't even have to suffer."

"You're a maniac. And an asshole."

"Yeah, so are you." I shot her a wicked look and blew smoke in her face. I could always get to her and make her laugh. She had always looked up to me, sort of as larger than life. Now she was gonna have to see me waste away. Poor kid.

About a week later, my oncologist told me he was going to try a new, experimental chemotherapy drug, along with radiation. I would do a cycle of chemo for several weeks as an outpatient. There was a novel's worth of side effects, but I decided to give it a try. My cough was just getting worse, and I was feeling more and more run down. I would have a short hospital stay after the chemo to be monitored, and then I could go on my way. I figured, what the hell. Nothing to lose.

Now when I got to the hospital, I had to chuckle. This mamaluke doc was telling me how to beat this thing, but meanwhile he weighed about 350 pounds! And I got the cancer after years of working out. Where was the justice in that? Not that I wished cancer on the guy, but give me a fuckin' break.

I'll tell you one thing, a hospital stay is no fuckin' picnic in the park. But during my two-day stay, one particular nurse cracked me up. I mean, I came in there as miserable as a person could get. I was in a bad way. The cough had me down for the count. I hadn't slept in days, even after drinking a couple bottles of wine. I wasn't right in my head, and I was depressed that I had the cancer and had to go through this shit. I was hooked up to machines and getting poked all over the fuckin' place for my intravenous cocktail. This place was cold and smelled like mothballs. I had magazines, but they were about as interesting as looking at the cracked, white paint on the walls. So yeah, I was a little grumpy and groggy. Sue me.

"So who do we have here? Mr. Joey it looks like," Nurse DuBois said.

She was a strong-looking woman, Jamaican with a slight accent. She had a kind face, but I was in no mood for her.

"What's a matter there? Your tail feather stuck to the bed, sir?" she crowed. "You need ta sit up and address me when I'm speakin' to ya, man."

I sat up, all right. I was thinking, *Is this bitch crazy, because I know she didn't talk to me like that!* I mean, I know I had no money and I wasn't in a nice hospital, but shit, I should get treated with respect just like anybody else.

I shot her a look. "You talkin' to me?"

"I knew that would get your attention, Mr. Joey." She peered down at me from small, square glasses. "I'm just bein' playful, meanin' no harm. You'd be surprised how many rooms I go into and how many patients give me no respect and pay me no mind. It hurts my feelin's, ya know."

"Yeah, I know," I answered. Now I could relate. "So you're it. Nurse DuBois's gonna see to it all my t's are crossed and i's are dotted while I'm here?"

"That's me," she said.

"Good."

She was cool and had a comforting way about her.

"By the way, my name is Wanda," she said. "That's what all my friends call me."

CHAPTER 11

NOTHING HAD CHANGED IN A week. I wasn't feeling better or worse, just nagged to death by Charo, who'd been breathing down my neck constantly about how I was feeling. One thing, though, she couldn't do enough for me. I could tell her to run to the store ten times a day, and she'd fuckin' do it. The tradeoff for that was her constant yakking about her family and her father, who lives downstairs. She lives with me, but I love being able to send her down to him when she starts getting on my nerves. I was actually looking forward to getting away and going to the hospital for my treatment.

As I got set up in a hospital room and then waited, I heard that familiar voice.

"So you're back for your treatment Mr. Joey?" Wanda asked. "How has the last week been to ya?"

"Oh, a fuckin' trill," I answered sarcastically.

"Now what kind of accent is that, Mr. Joey?"

"It's the dirty Bronx. And yes, the word is t-h-r-i-l-l, if I'm speakin the King's English like you, but get used to me, 'cause most of the fuckin' time I'm not."

"Oh, you're a riot, Mr. Joey. And yes, I do speak the King's English, as I am a Kingstonian, but I say trill and tree instead of three too." Her voice grew hushed. "But seriously, has anyone ever told you that your vocabulary is less than dignified?"

"Everyone, all the time."

We both laughed at that.

As she was prepping me for the needle, I thought maybe I could get some answers from her that the doc wouldn't provide. "So Wanda, what's your take on this poison? Ever see anyone get better on it?"

"I have." She paused. "But I've also seen people die shortly after it. How are you *feelin*? That's all that should matter to you right now, Mr. Joey."

"I actually didn't feel worse this week."

"Well then, that's something, isn't it?"

As I got to know her, I found her very intuitive. I wanted to get her take on my situation with Nina..

"Might even tell my daughter," I blurted out.

"No-man!" she exclaimed. "Don't tell me you haven't told your loved ones!" Her eyes widened and then narrowed as she peered at me. Her voice got stern. "Let me tell you, if I had a dime for every person who told me they didn't tell someone they loved dearly about their illness, well sir, I would be a rich woman today."

"Wonder what's stopping us," I asked, although I didn't need an answer.

"You're all cowards!" she laughed. "You've been given a label that you associate with death, and you let it take over your mind. Then you let it stop you from doin' and sayin' the things you want. And that is what I believe makes the sickness and the death come quicker. And besides, do you really think it won't leak out? You know how it goes, family members tell other family members, you start lookin' ill as the thing progresses. You're not being true, and your truth will eventually come out. We're all gonna die, man, most of us just don't dwell on it."

"Be lucky a doc hasn't given you a reason to feel this way," I answered her.

"And how did you say you were feelin' this week—not worse? So why you down, man? You're dwellin' on the label," Wanda said. "Call your daughter and tell her. If she's anything like you, she'll handle it."

"I hope so … for your sake, Wanda," I said sheepishly.

"Uh oh, Mr. Joey," Wanda said. "All this talk about your daughter and feelings and stuff, I almost forgot who I was talkin' to. You better not let that sappy stuff out again, I might forget what a badass you are."

"My word! Wanda, are you cursing?" I said coyly. "What's happenin' to the two of us?"

"We're rubbing off on each other, that's what," she said. "I just hope my advice sticks. Call the girl. You need her right now."

Wanda left to see another patient. When she returned to my room, I told her all about Nina and our relationship. She gave me good advice that day. I decided to call my daughter.

It's funny, but I actually started feeling better when I left my treatment. I had no nasty side effects, just a headache and nausea, some fatigue. I started to think that maybe I could actually beat this thing. Now all I had to do was make it through another three weeks and see if the cancer was shrinking. But I wasn't going to wait till then to tell Nina. That was next on my list.

So when I arrived home and Charo casually told me Joanne had called and told Nina my news, I was pissed.

"What do you mean she fuckin' told Nina?" I shouted. "Give me that fuckin' phone."

"Oh sweetie, baby, please calm down before you call her," Charo begged.

"Just give me the phone so I can find out what the hell she said."

As I started coughing my brains out midway through my fit, Charo insisted on dialing for me and gave me the phone.

"Yeah, Joanne, what the fuck? You told Nina I was sick?" I asked.

"Now Joey, I know you're mad, but just listen to me," she warned.

"No, you listen to me!" I yelled. "Maybe you should've thought about clearing this with me. I mean, I'm not fuckin' dead yet. I can speak for myself, goddamnit. This is news I should've told my daughter myself."

"Okay, but just hear me out," Joanne said. "I was talking to her, and she started asking me how you were feeling. She started talking about you 'being so sick' and how you guys talking is so great, especially during this time of your life. So I said, 'so you know about him being sick?' and she said, 'yeah of course.' So I asked if she was taking it okay and she goes, 'what do you mean?' At that point I knew I was in trouble. There was this dead silence. It was like she instantly knew without me saying a word."

"Yeah and then what?" I said angrily, but I was eager to hear about Nina's reaction.

"Well, she said she was talking about your bronchitis but she feared it was something more. When I actually said the word *cancer*, she flooded me with questions, almost how I was with you when I found out. She has the best intentions for you. At that point I told her she had better talk to you about it. I didn't want to tell her how bad it really is."

"Oh, well, gee, thanks," I said sarcastically. "Is she expecting me to call her today?"

"I think you better."

So that's exactly what I did. I figured I might as well throw some salt on a fresh wound. Don't get me wrong—somewhere in the back of my mind I hoped I was going to get better or somehow just live with the thing. I mean, I couldn't grasp that I was going to die sooner rather than later. I had been through a lot in my fifty-nine years and always made it through. Yet, the way it looked on paper was that death was imminently close. I had to man-up and tell her the ugly truth.

"Hello, Nina," I said softly.

"Hi, Dad." She got right to the point. "I want the truth. How bad is it?"

"It's not fuckin' good, that's for sure," I said. "The doc told me I got about six months."

"How long ago did he tell you that? Did you know this when you first contacted me at Christmas?"

"No ... shortly after, though. It's been a month since I found out, and I've actually had two chemo treatments already."

Silence.

"Hello? Yo, Neen," There was just dead air. I could only assume she was crying.

"I'm here," she said somberly. "I just can't believe how unfair this is, for both of us. It's like someone is playing a joke. I'm sorry to sound this way. I just thought things would be different, especially now that we're back in each other's lives. You have a grandchild you haven't even met yet, for God's sake. I thought we would have a chance to make up for all the lost time."

"Me too, me too," I agreed.

We sat on the phone in silence. Seconds seemed like minutes, and minutes seemed like an hour.

And that was it. After that conversation, I could tell she put up a strong façade. She certainly was a trouper, and she filled every conversation with me with hope. She had a never-say-die attitude. She must have gotten that from me. Good kid, tough kid.

So the week went by, and I started to experience the reactions to the treatment I thought I had escaped. Every day was a new adventure in discomfort or pain. I couldn't pee, I shit my brains out one night, and another night I had the double pleasure of throwing up and shitting at the same time. After that, anyone would be weak, but I still had this cough that was tearing up my chest. It was guttural and just plain gross. So the next day I was off to the hospital for my treatment, and I planned to tell the doctor to stop the treatments. I had only two left anyway.

Waiting in the hospital room always gave me a cold and eerie feeling. I hated it. I couldn't stand the sight or the smells, never could. Whenever anyone I knew was in the hospital I rarely ever went to visit.

I remember when I was admitted to the hospital after my attempt at ending it all with dog tranquilizers. That shit couldn't kill me, but the hospital stay almost did. The fuckin' doctors had me strapped to the bed and were shocking me. My sister and Caroline came to see me. I felt like a caged animal that everyone pitied. I had hit my lowest point and felt as though they were all happy to see their hero fall, as if that was what I deserved. They made me feel I was beneath them. They didn't do anything in particular; it was just the way I felt. They did try to make me laugh a couple times. I don't know, maybe I was just paranoid at the time. Of course, I don't feel that way about my sister now, but Caroline—who knows? She was probably wishing bad shit on me for years. It's the past. What ya gonna do?

"So doc, listen," I summoned Dr. Danziger. I referred to him as Dr. D, and Dr. Death, among other things. "I think I'm done with all this treatment bullshit."

"Oh, I'm sorry to hear that, Mr. Martino, because you still have one more after this one," he replied casually.

"Yeah, well, it's not workin' out too good, if ya know what I mean. Been real sick and shit."

"I see, but that is to be expected. You may have to have someone stay with you this last week if you think you can't handle it."

"I got Charo," I told him. And he knew that.

"No, I mean someone professional, like a nurse, who could help you when things get, uh, rough."

"No way, doc. The only nurse I want to see is Wanda, Nurse DuBois. Where is she, by the way?"

"She took a couple of days off, some family emergency," he muttered.

"Oh, damn, I was really looking forward to seeing her. Will she be back next week?"

"Should be," he mumbled. "Listen, Joey, buck up for one more week. I know these treatments can get unpleasant, but I am going to send you downstairs for an MRI to see if there has been a change in your condition. Whatever the case, I will see you next week, got it?"

"Yeah, yeah, got it."

The fuck had the personality of a fly. He was textbook all the way, but he was all I had. I had to trust him, so I would do the scan and sweat it out another week. Besides, Nina was banking on me getting better.

I was mostly alone in my one-room apartment, and I didn't leave that room the whole next week. Half the time I slept on the floor. I was so weak, and the cough was relentless. I would lie on the wood floor, and every time I coughed, it vibrated against the grain like a drum. It drove me crazy. The cough would build into such a crescendo it felt as though my lungs would burst into a million pieces. At times I just wanted my lungs to explode or leave my body. That week was a blur. I showered only once, with Charo's assistance. I even had to start depending on her helping me whenever I had to go to the bathroom. What was happening? How could I be losing control like this?

Nina was good about calling to check on me, and Joanne was keeping her current on what was happening with the treatments. I could tell Nina hated having to speak to Charo, though, so I told her to call me at night, around 11:30. Charo usually was not there at that time. I like to watch the news, so right about 11:00 Charo would usually go see her father downstairs. I usually wouldn't see her until the next morning.

Charo got the vibe that Nina didn't want to speak with her. This bothered her.

"Joey, babee, why you dawta don't talk to me so much?" she moaned.

"She only just recently started talking to me," I said. "What, you want her to have an hour-long conversation with you?"

"I just wanna know her a leetle bit. Why she don't wanna know me, Joey?"

"I don't know, get over it. It's not important."

"Are ju saying I'm no importante?"

"No! Jesus Christ, I'm sick and dying over here, and this is what you care about?" I knew if I carried on a little and used "Jesus Christ" she would shut up. She hated when I used God's name as an expletive. "Next time she calls, I'll tell her you want to talk to her, okay? Would that make you happy, dear?"

"Jes, it would."

"Good, case closed."

Finally the aggravation was over. The truth was, Nina could never understand my relationship with Charo. I had figured that out that the day she met Charo, just by the comments she had made at the social club. But I had never been able to explain it to her, either.

When I first met Charo, I was married to another woman named Fran. I started seeing Fran almost immediately after Patti and I broke up. It was a total rebound relationship for me. Getting married was a spontaneous decision. I never really took the commitment seriously even though I went into it with good intentions. Charo was a fixture at this bar I used to go to in the Bronx. She knew Tony Bo and some other goombas of mine. She was flamboyant, and at first I found her a little bizarre, but that turned me on. I always had a penchant for wild broads—the wilder and weirder the better.

Charo had slept with a couple of the guys from the bar; basically, if you could give her a meal and some snow, she would blow you like nobody's business. Those days I was up for anything, plus I was pretty much done with the "married thing," and one night she made a move. She came and sat on the bar stool next to me, and we started chatting. I never understood much of what she said back then, but she'd always laugh her ass off at my stories. I had heard she liked me, so I wasn't surprised when she started stroking my hair and then put her other hand on my leg. Before I knew it, she was grabbing my crotch, pretty aggressively. She had big hands, and I liked her forcefulness. I didn't have to understand her when she spoke to know what she was after.

I was feeling right, nothing stopping me, so I took her back to the car. She stroked me the whole way to the car, and I was hard as a rock. She went down on me immediately, and I couldn't see anything past her big blonde wig covering my shit. All I know is that night she gave me one of the best hummers I'd had in a long time. I gave her some blow after I shot my load, and she supplied me with everything I needed after that. She spoiled me, what can I say. Now, how could I tell that story to Nina?

When Nina called that night, I told her about Charo wanting to talk to her more, and she just laughed.

"Well, I don't think we'll become buddies, let's put it that way," she said.

I didn't blame her, and I didn't want to push it. You never knew what Charo might tell her. She could be a loose cannon.

This time when she asked me how I was feeling, I couldn't lie. The cough started in every time I tried to answer her.

"You sound horrible," she said. "I wish there were something I could do. It's so frustrating being so far away, knowing you're going through this. I just can't leave the baby yet, and I don't feel comfortable putting him on a plane."

"I know, I know, it's okay," I calmed her. "You got a lot of responsibilities down there."

I couldn't blame her for her ambivalence about traveling, especially after 9/11. She definitely seemed to have grown into a very responsible girl. Besides, I was embarrassed to let her see me like this.

"Do you know if the cancer is shrinking at all?" she asked.

"I should know something tomorrow when I go for treatment. I got to go though, hon, I'm real tired tonight."

I didn't want to give her the details of my battles. I knew she was worried.

"Well, keep your chin up," she said. "Hopefully you'll get good news tomorrow. I'll be praying for you."

"I'll let ya know. Love ya."

CHAPTER 12

WHEN I WOKE UP, I felt okay, though any moment I could take a breath and double over coughing. But for the most part I was okay. I also knew there was a chance I'd see Wanda today. I knew she had been away on an "emergency" last time, so when I walked into the hospital I bought her a fake red velvet rose from the gift shop. It was all I could afford, even after borrowing money from Charo before I left the house.

This visit, Joanne was going to pick up Charo to meet me here and take me home. On the plus side, I wouldn't have to ride home in that musty, old, hospital courtesy van that I once used to shuttle me back and forth. The negative was that both women would both be there to grill Dr. D and anyone else they could corner.

When I got to the hospital I asked if Wanda was working. I was told that she was, and I asked to be on her rotation. When she finally walked in the room, I felt calm.

"Wow!" she exclaimed. "You're actually crackin' a smile. You must have missed me."

"You? Never!" I said and rolled my eyes. "I did bring you somethin', though, on the off chance that you would be here." As I handed her the rose, I asked if everything was all right.

"Oh, my gosh!" she cried. "Mr. Joey, that is so sweet of you. Thank you, you ol' softy. See I knew it, deep down. But to answer your question, yes, everything is fine, my dear."

"They told me that you had an emergency," I said inquisitively.

"Oh, my, yes," she said. "But for the most joyous of events. My daughter had a baby girl. The water broke unexpectedly, so I had to just pick up my things and go, man. It's a miraculous event, you know, to see your baby have a baby."

"Well, good, good for you," I said with a little envy.

"This is my fifth grandbaby, Mr. Joey, and every one of them is special. I can proudly say I haven't missed a birth. The birth of a child is truly a miracle from God, and when you have a chance to witness it, well, it's just awesome, Mr. Joey."

"I bet," I said.

I thought any minute she was gonna start gushing. I sort of thought it would have been nice to see my grandson being born. But I didn't, so I couldn't look back now.

"You know, Wanda, I remember how I felt when I found out Nina was pregnant," I told her. I wanted to relate to her. "I guess it was sort of that way, you know, with you and your grandkids.

"But I couldn't help feelin' sad, too" I continued. "It was right after 9/11. It was like the world was goin' to shit, excuse my French, and now she was gonna bring a kid into this mess. I felt bad for thinkin' like that, but everyone was sad and depressed about stuff then. Where were you when it happened?"

"Oh my, I was right here, Mr. Joey," she said solemnly. "Everyone was so scared here. Patients in bed who heard about it were crying, shouting out. They were beggin' us to dial numbers for them to check on loved ones. Everyone on staff that day stayed to help. Some of us went to the main roads to see if anyone needed assistance as they were walkin' home from the City. It was horrible. It looked like a mass exodus of zombies. Lots of people were covered in ash, disheveled, and confused. I could never have imagined such a day. Such tragedy. We lost a lot of good people that day, Mr. Joey."

"Don't I know it!" I said. "Just look at all those poor people and their families. Sometimes when I'm lookin' out my window, I can still smell the smoke and ash. I can remember that day so clearly. Maybe I'm better off dead if that's what the world is coming to. What a fuckin' day. I'll never get it out of my mind. I woke up to chaos. Charo shaking me and screamin' at the tops of her lungs, *'Joey wake up, WAKE UP!! Oh Jesus help us, Please Gods!*

"She sounds very animated, Mr. Joey," Wanda said. "But I know everyone was going out of control that day, man."

"So I asked why the fuck she was shaking me and told her to calm down. Then she told me what the hell was going on, that a plane had flown into a building. I said to myself, *Holy shit!* I just stood there in shock watching the TV. A million things were goin' through my head. More than anything else I felt dread. The city that I love—hell that we all love—was under attack. Then boom, the second tower was hit, and then I thought, what building is gonna be next? Hell, America was under attack. How could this be happenin'?"

"I know, I know Mr. Joey." She nodded solemnly. "It just seemed inconceivable."

"When the towers fell, my heart sank. I felt like I couldn't breathe, because there was nothin' I could do about it. I felt numb, like someone was drainin' all the life out of me. It was so damn depressing. The following days, my sister took me downtown with her—you know as close as they would let us go—and we sat there makin' sandwiches for the firefighters. Well, okay, she made the sandwiches, and I commiserated with them. But it was crazy, the unity we all felt.

"I tell ya, Wanda, the world is fucked up, and full of fucked-up people. The funny thing is, on a day like that you think of the people who mean the most to you and where they are. Are they safe, scared, what? I thought of Nina. I hoped Scott was taking care of her and comforting her."

I paused to think about Nina as a little kid.

"For some reason, though, as she started maturing through the years, I never really worried about her. I always knew she would be okay no matter what."

"So many things you have told me Mr. Joey," Wanda interrupted. "You mean you didn't show concern through the years? For goodness sake, she is a girl."

"I mean I'm not the worrying type anyway, but this was different," I defended myself. I didn't want her to think I didn't care about my daughter.

"She had a calm way about her, and through everything she always managed to land on her feet. Who knows why she's tough. Maybe it's just how she acts with me. I used to worry more when she was little, and becomin' a teenager too. I don't really know why I stopped worryin'. Maybe it was because she didn't appreciate my displays of concern, so I stopped."

"What you mean by 'displays of concern,' Mr. Joey?" she asked. "Oh, Lord, knowin' what I know of you, I can just imagine."

I shot Wanda a look and then explained.

"I'll never forget the couple of times I had to threaten to kick some chump's ass for coming too close for comfort. One time I even had to show a guy my gun. I mean what are these guys, nuts? Whenever they saw me comin' they fuckin' ran for the hills. Ha, one kid nearly shit his pants. Good for him, fuck 'em."

"Sounds to me like you were a loose cannon," Wanda said. "No wonder the girl never wanted to worry you. She was probably afraid of what you might do … much less embarrassed."

"Listen, she could be embarrassed all she wants," I retorted. "And as for fear, it's good she had some fear. That's what kids are missin' these days. Whatever it did, if anything, it was worth it. She's here in one piece to tell the stories, and she didn't wind up with any rat bastards."

Just then I started coughing unmercifully. Nothing seemed to calm it. Wanda got me water, and tried rubbing my back. I excused myself and tried to produce some phlegm. Wanda heard me and came into the bathroom unexpectedly. I really didn't want her to see what was in the bowl.

"Oh my dear, you have to let it out easier," she said. "Hmm, hmm, this is not too good."

She was referring to the blood the bowl.

"How often are you producin' blood?"

"Most of the time. I thought maybe it was a side-effect from the treatment."

"Could be, but not for you, Mr. Joey," she said. She stared at me. "Do you remember you said you were havin' this problem before I met you? With your condition it is called hemoptysis. Is this worse than before?"

"Worse, better, I don't know," I snapped. "It's all the same to me."

She backed off. "Well now, Mr. Joey, I think that's all the talkin' for today," she said. "You need to rest. I will get you propped up on the bed here comfortably until the doctor arrives. No worries, Mr. Joey."

Some time passed, and I dozed off into a deep sleep, probably some of the best sleep I'd had in a while—until the Grim Reaper woke me up.

"Mr. Martino, are you awake?" Dr. D asked as he put his meat hook on my shoulder.

"Now I am, unfortunately," I answered. I hate to be disturbed when I'm sleeping.

"Well, good, because we have some important things to discuss."

His voice was stern. He cleared his throat, laid out some test results on the table next to the bed, including scans and X-rays, and then continued.

"This all tells a story. As in any story there is both good and bad; things are not usually plain and simple, because then it would not be a very interesting story."

"What is this, *kindeegarten*? Just get to it. It's fine; I'm a big boy. I can take it."

After more of the doc's mumbo jumbo, he finally cut to the chase and spoke in sentences I could understand.

"Joey, what this indicates is that your body has responded well to the treatment in regards to the lungs. The tumors have slowed and in some cases, stopped growing. However, your lungs, specifically the alveoli, are very diseased from the years of nicotine abuse, and your breathing is very labored. This is why it is hard for you to catch your breath, especially when you are coughing. This is not going to go away, even if the cancer was completely gone. Now, this is disturbing here. Do you see this?"

I had hope until this wise guy started pointing his finger at this one particular X-ray.

"Yeah, I see it. And what exactly am I looking at?"

"This right here is a spot." He pointed out. "And here is another one. Notice they are all on your bones."

Now, sure they could have been benign, but me not being stupid, plus the fact that I had cancer, I think it was safe to assume I now had bone cancer. The doctor confirmed this a few seconds later, but called it metastatic lung cancer. The doctor explained that lung cancer would always be the name of any cancer I got, since that was where it started. Even so, how could this be? The doctor went on to explain that even though I was receiving treatment, it was treatment for one type of cancer. This thing was taking over. It was like a war inside my body. I was being fired upon, and then the cancer decided to take hold somewhere else and metastasize. Lucky me.

As for further treatment, the doc laid out lots of plans, like a second round of chemo that could be done in five days, and radiation treatment. However, I told the doctor I was done. Let the chips fall where they may. But that would be *our* secret.

Before we ended our meeting I asked if he could get Wanda for me. When she walked in, I wanted to let her know I was okay for now.

"So, Mr. Joey, tell me something good."

"Okay … Good & Plenty is my favorite candy!" I chuckled out of frustration. "That's about the only *good* I can think of right now, Wanda, since the doc came by and just told me a horror story. Yeah, maybe you've heard of it—it's called metastatic lung cancer, and I have it. Seems that it is my reward after all these weeks of lovely treatments."

"Oh my, I am truly sorry to hear that, Mr. Joey," she said empathetically. "Where do we go from here?"

"Jamaica, the Bahamas, Cancun?" I joked, and she laughed. "Somewhere fuckin' tropical. Oh Wanda, seriously, I'd give anything to be on a beach, preferably Florida, soakin' up the sun, you know? Away from all this shit."

"I know man, I hear ya!" she said heartily. She paused as she tidied up the room. "So are you gonna start radiation? Second round chemo? I know the usual recommendations. What did the oncologist suggest for you, Mr. Joey?"

I waited a minute before I answered. *Do I tell her what she wants to hear, or do I give it to her straight?* She had been a real good sport, listenin' to all my stories these past weeks. Plus, she was probably the only non-relative friend I had. She can handle it.

"Wanda, I'm almost sixty years old, and truth be told, I am nowhere," I started. "You think what you're seein' is the way I always used to be?"

"No man, I've heard your stories," she said.

"Right, and they were true," I explained. "I always had my health, looks, women, and at times, money. I've let everything slip away, and not on purpose. Hell, even my family was gone up until recently. And I think that's because I'm sick now and they feel sorry for me. Otherwise, no one would want to be around me. Maybe I pissed my sister off one too many times, who the hell knows. But really, that's how it's been for me. I only just started talking to Nina again. I mean, what can I offer anyone at this point? I don't want to be a burden."

And then it hit me.

"You know what's really funny? I guess I'm realizin' at this very moment that I never really thought about what *I* could offer anyone. Before, when I had all those *things* to offer, I didn't think about giving. But now that I got nothin', I'm desperate to get just one thing back—anything—so I could give it away. So I would be worth somethin' to somebody."

"Mr. Joey, everyone is worth something," Wanda said gently. "And you are worth more than you know."

"Wanda, that's kind of you to say. But besides you, no one really knows me, not anymore. And you know what? I don't want to be one of those fuckin' people who die and other people come just to gawk. Seriously, you see this a lot with old people and people like me who are dying of a disease. Most of the people who come to see you at the end, they talk to you about trivial bullshit, and when you're gone. they act like you were best buddies. I hate that shit. And I'm guilty of that shit. We all are. We don't take the time to care or really know the person who's on the way out. We placate, we coddle, and we patronize the old, the sick and the dying. Maybe we do it as a society because we don't want to open ourselves up for the hurt that inevitably will come if we allow a real relationship to take place. Who the hell knows? All I know is that I don't want to be on the receiving end of that shit."

Wanda sat down beside me. "Mr. Joey what you are sayin' is wise," she said. "Unfortunately, we can't change human nature. In my business, I have to keep my defenses up even more, because I see many come and go. But I keep giving compassion and an ear. Gettin' to know people is my reward, even if it is for a short time. Look at yourself. You've made me laugh and made my days here very jolly. I'm thankful for you. I'm hoping you decide to fight this thing. After all, I want to keep seeing you."

"Yeah, me too, me too," I acknowledged. "You're the only thing that keeps me comin' back to this rotten joint."

"That's nice to hear, because nobody ever wants to see me, man, especially when I come pushing in with my cart of needles," Wanda said. "But I know you. You like to see me too."

She started to walk out but turned back and said, "Mr. Joey ... try not to give up."

I put my hand up as if to wave and with a nod I whispered, "We'll see."

When she left the room, I got really cold. I wondered if I was ever going to see her again. Funny, but it was all I could think about for the rest of the day, especially after the grim diagnosis. And it's all I kept thinking about even during the car ride home with Joanne and Charo, and, believe me, they wouldn't shut up. Luckily for the doc, they hadn't been able to track him down. So I kept things short and simple for them as they asked me what he had to say. I wanted to give them as little information as possible otherwise they would've talked my ear off.

But I still couldn't shake this weird feeling. I started realizing that all my encounters with people could be my last. It seemed like a bad dream. The more I thought about it, the more confused I got. Was I never going to see anyone again, or were they just not going to see me? Would I be looking either up or down at people, or would I be in hell for all my sins? Would I be reincarnated and get to see everything I wanted in a new body? Who the frig knew. Would anybody be able to tell me in the last seconds of my life? Would I ride forever on my Harley Davidson, at peace, or would I suffer, damned for all eternity? One thing was for sure, I'd sure as shit better talk to a priest before I kicked the bucket.

When I got home I got a big surprise as I listened to my answering machine. It was probably the last good surprise I'd ever get. Nina was coming to see me! She was bringing my grandson.

I was happy inside but incredibly nervous, imagining her reaction when she saw me. I mean, it had been so many years, and I wasn't looking too good. Did I really want her to remember me like this?

All I knew was that I wanted to see her. I wanted to make amends in person.

CHAPTER 13

TODAY I WILL MEET MY grandson for the first time, I thought. What a trip.

The plan was for Joanne to pick up Nina and baby Jack at the airport and then drive them directly here to my apartment. Charo was excited too, but I decided to have her visit with her father downstairs and leave me alone for this first visit. I felt Nina would want it that way.

I'd gotten used to my newest companion, a motorized wheelchair that Joanne delivered to me a week ago. I was not too steady on my feet and this got me around pretty quickly, but as I was sitting in it, I realized Nina might be a little shocked to see me this way. I couldn't dwell on it, though. It is what it is, so what ya gonna do?

Just then the phone rang. It was Joanne.

She told me everyone had gotten in safely and they were on their way. "But listen, I forgot to tell you one thing," she said.

"What's that?" I couldn't imagine what it was. Couldn't be any big deal, I figured.

"I forgot to tell you that Caroline is with them."

"You're kiddin'," I said, surprised.

This caught me off guard. I mean, no way was I expecting her to come. I guessed I really must be dying, for her to want to see me. Now I really felt self-conscious. But there was nothing I could do.

"Are you okay with it?" she asked. "I mean, I'm sorry I forgot to tell you, everything just happened so fast."

"Yeah, yeah. Well, tell her not to expect Don Juan," I joked. "I'll see yas when you get here."

My place was a mess, and so it would stay. All I really owned was a small metal wall unit with an old hi-fi, a snack table, and a mattress, which was on the floor now because sometimes I couldn't make it out of bed to get to the bathroom when I was sick from the chemo.

Charo had a small kitchenette table and chairs where we ate our meals. Luckily, Joanne had given me a television and video player, which kept me very occupied. One of our neighbor's little boy would come over some afternoons to watch Disney videos with me. Lately that and reading had been my only sources of entertainment.

My videos, along with my Beatles albums, were the most valuable things I owned. Oh yeah, and a pinky ring with a blue sapphire in it that I mostly wore in my heyday. Any self-respecting goodfella has to have a pinky ring. Nina used to admire the ring, and I figured I'd give it to her.

I used to love jewelry: gold chains from Italy, crosses and Italian horns, watches, big rings. All of it was gone—hocked. I had to do what I had to do. Sad, though; I really had nothing to give Nina, nothing to hand down. Never thought about being in this situation, I always just lived for the day at hand. I thought I was invincible, and now that I knew I wasn't, I was shit out of luck.

"Oh shit!" I said out loud.

I must have dozed off. They would be here any minute. I at least wanted to make myself a little presentable, put on a clean, white T-shirt and comb my hair. I hobbled into the bathroom and got myself ready as best I could. When I was done, I sat back down in my wheelchair and I caught a glimpse of my image in the mirror leaning against the wall. I knew I looked different. My Coke-bottle glasses didn't help things any. Oh well, what ya gonna do.

Just then the bell rang, and I buzzed them in. Suddenly my palms were sweaty. I wheeled myself over to the door and left it open for them. Then I wheeled myself back to the table, facing the door, so I could see them as they walked in.

I heard something. The elevator. Joanne's voice. Their voices. And there I was. Face to face with two people who were once the biggest part of my life. I had a lump in my throat.

"Hi!" Nina led the greetings.

"How ya doin today, Joey?" asked Joanne.

Caroline just stood there and smiled politely, like a schoolgirl.

"Good, good," I answered. "How you guys doing? Sit, sit, don't be shy. My, who is this little guy here?"

"This is Jack, your grandson," Nina said.

She asked Jack in a baby voice if he knew I was his grandpa. She asked him if he would like to give me a hug. He seemed a little unsure, probably because of the chair.

"Sure, you know what, put him on my lap," I encouraged. "Don't be afraid of the chair," I told the child. "These are my wheels. I do some of my best driving in this thing."

I felt awkward holding him, mostly because I didn't want to drop him, but I was in awe of him. I touched his hair and his little face. I looked into his eyes and realized the resemblance.

"He's definitely a Martino," I said. Then for some reason I gave a hearty laugh.

They sat next to me. We made some small talk, and everyone said I looked good. What a lie. Joanne decided to do a little food run for me while I visited with Nina and Caroline. At that moment, Caroline got up, and scooped up Jack. Caroline took Jack and said they would join Joanne on her shopping trip.

Joanne leaned down beside me and said in a low tone, "I think some alone time would be good for the two of you."

So there I was, alone with Nina. I couldn't remember the last time we were in the same room together, no less alone.

"This is nice," I started.

"Yes, yes it is."

"So, what's up, kid? You look good. Keeping yourself well down there in sunny F-L-A?"

"Yep, it's definitely my home now." She hesitated. "I like what you've done with the chair."

She was funny, good sense of humor, that kid. She was referring to the black shirt I had over the backrest of my chair. It had "PATCO" written in large white letters across it.

"Once an air traffic controller, always one, is that it?" she said.

"You got that right," I said, lighting a cigarette. That seemed to change her mood a little.

"C'mon, are you serious," she asked in disbelief. "How could you be smoking after everything?"

"What, you'd deny me the only enjoyment I got left in life?"

"That little enjoyment is what's killing you! I can't believe you. I have been so concerned about you. I came all this way in the snow, with the baby, and you're smoking right in front of me."

"A, oh! I'm just bein' me," I exclaimed. "I gotta be me, Nina."

She smiled a little and then looked down. I noticed her glancing at all the prescriptions lined up on my kitchen table. She started playing with the bottles and then reached for a pen in her purse. She grabbed a scrap piece of paper and wrote down all the names of the pills and asked me what they were for. What a disaster. I had to reveal that I couldn't even take a normal piss anymore. She wrote it all down in a fury, as if trying to finish a timed test. She mumbled something about wanting to keep tabs on the doctors and make sure I was getting the right medicines without mixing them up. She meant well, and she was in robot mode, so I let her have at it.

Nina couldn't tell but I was really staring at her through my reading glasses. I was studying everything about her—how she looked, her mannerisms, even her unpolished fingernails. She used to have long, fake fingernails, and she used to wear lots of jewelry and makeup, with her hair all teased up high. Now, though, she was pretty and wore only the simplest makeup; she was surprisingly plain, maybe because she had become a mom. She'd always had a cute little body. She worked out, and it showed. I took the credit for showing her the ropes about exercise. Maybe that was something of me that would live on in her. I was trying to take a mental snapshot, as if I could take this moment with me.

Then she stopped writing and looked at me.

"How come you never called?" Nina asked solemnly. "Did you ever think about me in all this time?"

"Of course," I answered.

I was never good at this deep emotional shit, probably because I never wanted to lose my cool and start crying or have a breakdown in front of anybody, especially her.

"I felt you were better off. You know, given my situation and shit."

"What situation?" she asked suspiciously. She probably meant *which* situation.

"You know, Charo, my living situation, my health issues, have your pick. You know, I got the message when you didn't invite me to your wedding."

"I figured you wouldn't come."

We stared at each other for a minute.

I broke the silence. "You could've picked up the phone too, you know."

"I'm sorry. I let so much time go by." Nina lowered her eyes.

"Me too, me too," I acknowledged.

"It all seems pointless now," she said, looking back up at me. "I want you to know that I'm here now, and I want to do the right thing by you, you know, in the end. We should talk about things. Be real and get things in order. Like ... um, how do you want to go? What do you want me to do for you after you are gone?"

"Gettin' right to it, huh?"

"Well, I want to know a lot of things but for right now, this is very important. Have you given it any thought?"

"I'm still fightin' the good fight, you know," I said. "Maybe one day, if all this changes, I'll get down to see you."

I paused and looked away. Then I attacked her question with a fury. She didn't know, but I had thought about my demise many times. I just never thought I would ever get to tell anyone who could do it for me. I mean, I guess I thought I would die suddenly or in an accident, and I wouldn't even get to have this conversation. But now that the question was being asked, I knew what I wanted to say. What's more, I knew Nina could handle it.

As I leaned forward and put out my cigarette, I confidently told her my wishes.

"I want to be cremated, and I don't want to stick around long," I started. "I want to be divided in trees."

"You mean threes," she corrected.

"Yeah, don't get cute."

"It's between you, Charo, and my sister and brother."

"That's more than three, you know," Nina said.

"Yeah I know. I figure they'll either divide that third up, or Joanne will just keep 'em. Anyway, whenever you see fit, I want my ashes to be scattered in St. Augustine, off the Bridge of Lyons. I've always loved it there. It has everything I love: it's on the water, a bustling town, big motorcycle hangout, bars, restaurants, great food, Spanish culture ...

and the history with the fort is just amazing. You know I love that shit, and I was down there a couple of years ago with Charo, taking it all in."

I probably shouldn't have told her that part.

"You came all the way down to Florida, and you didn't call me?" she acted stunned.

"It was a quick trip, and besides, you and I weren't talking, and I didn't feel you would've wanted to see me anyway. It doesn't matter."

"I guess not."

"Well, that's my wish, although I suspect Charo will wanna keep my ashes, and that's fine. She's a pain in the ass, but I know she really loves me. Anyway, you okay with all this? I trust you more than anyone. You know that, right?"

"Yeah."

"There's something else," I said seriously. "You know I'm a fighter and all that shit. But I definitely don't want to suffer or be kept alive and not have any quality of life."

"So you want a DNR? You know, do not resuscitate."

"Yeah, yeah, that thing." I knew she would be on my wavelength. "I don't want everyone gawkin' over me, especially in that state. When it's time, it's time. And I don't want you cryin', you hear? You got responsibilities that you got to worry about."

"I have responsibilities, yes, but I still have feelings too," Nina answered.

Then she looked down for a minute, and when she looked up her eyes had welled up. A tear fell, and I instinctively put my hand out across the table to her. But she didn't take it. Instead, she got up and sat in my lap in the wheelchair and wrapped her arms around me. I quietly sobbed on the inside, coughing as I tried to hold in my tears. The lump in my throat was too big. I was afraid to say anything. Her body quivered with her almost silent crying. I knew I had to say something to try to calm her down. I was never good at this.

"Shh, Nina, shh. It's gonna be okay," I told her. "I love you, ya know."

"I know," she said quietly as she composed herself and got up. "I'm just stealing a moment with you. I'm glad we had this time."

"Me too," I agreed.

"We're kind of lucky, I guess," she went on. "Some people never get time to express how they feel."

She got up to blow her nose and get me some water. After that, we talked for a few more minutes about my treatments, the oncologist, and my friendship with Wanda. Before I knew where the time had gone, Joanne, Jack, and Caroline walked in.

"Hi, guys!" Joanne exclaimed. "Is everything good here?"

"Yes, yes, of course," Nina said.

I nodded. "She's a good kid."

"That's for sure," Caroline agreed. "The best!"

When they left, I felt unusually lonely. It was a gray day, and I knew the next time I saw Nina, I would probably be in the hospital. I just hoped I would even know she was there.

CHAPTER 14

THE COLD FLOOR FELT GOOD against my skin. I was limp and sweaty. I had rolled off the bed and couldn't get back up. My body was in pain from vomiting, and I couldn't take a deep breath without coughing or spitting up blood.

Now, when I talked, it was practically a whisper, and it had been only a week since I'd seen Nina, two months since I was given my death sentence. Lucky me—according to the doctor, I still had four more months of this shit.

Yeah, the floor was nice. *I think I'll stay here.* And off to sleep I went ... for a little while.

"Uh, ughh, I'm so c-cold. I n-need a fuckin' blanket s-s-somebody, Ch-Charo, where are you?"

I grabbed the phone and dialed Charo while I shivered. Nobody answered. I dialed a different number the next time.

"Nina, I need you, I need your help," I said.

"Hello, hello? I can't hear you. Dad? Is that you?"

"Nina, I know you can't hardly hear me, but I'm so cold." I needed to hear another human voice.

"It's one a.m.! Are you in your apartment alone?" she asked.

"I'm just so c-cold. I fell out of the b-bed. I'm on the floor," I explained.

"Oh, my gosh!" she exclaimed. "Listen, you have to hang up with me and try to call Charo at her father's. You need to get warm."

"I tried her already ... I think I'm dyin'..."

"No, don't say that," she shouted and then quieted her voice. "My gosh, okay, listen to me. You are going to pull yourself up onto that mattress and get those covers on. Do you hear me?"

"I can't, I'm cold."

"You are delirious, and you're suffering from all the chemo. This will be over soon. You need to grab the end of the mattress and get one leg and one arm propped on it and hoist yourself up. You are right next to the bed, aren't you?"

"Yeah."

"Crawl up if you can. You have to try. You are stronger than this. Do it, while I stay on the phone with you," she commanded.

Nina patiently talked me through every step of getting back into bed, though I didn't think I had enough strength. It was excruciating. Finally, I made it.

"Ugh, I wish I was in Florida," I dreamed out loud. "It's nice and warm and sunny there."

When I woke up the next morning, the phone was off the hook and I was sprawled out, almost naked, on the mattress.

"Joeee, *ay Dios mio*, my babee!" Charo exclaimed. "I cannot believe I did not hear the phone ring. Yoanna called me dis morning to tell me about what happen last night with ju and Nina. I'm sooo sorry, sweetie. Oh, ju poor thing."

I had to think for a minute, and then I realized I never hung up the phone or finished talking to Nina. It was like a bad fever. I was sweating my brains out one minute and then shivering the next. Once I got back onto the bed, I probably just collapsed from exhaustion. I hope I hadn't freaked her out.

"Yeah, yeah, calm down," I said hurriedly. "I'm fine. How's the kid? I hope I didn't scare her."

"No, babee, she was very concerned for ju," she said. "That's what Yoanna tell me."

"I better give her a call today."

"No, it's okay," Charo said. "I checked on ju while I was talking to Yoanna, and then Yoanna called Nina to tell her ju were okay."

"Good."

But I also thought I should call Nina myself. After her visit, I actually got to thinking that I might try another route of therapy. But this week the effects of the chemo seemed to really be kicking my ass. I might have to reconsider, or at least wait until I felt somewhat human again.

That night I was bad again—throwing up too. Charo stayed with me this time and made sure I was okay. I was like this for a couple more days. It was like being on a roller coaster ride I couldn't get off. I just wanted to feel normal again. I also had the nagging urge to fight this thing, but I just couldn't deal with all the extra crap that came with the fight.

I spoke to Nina a couple of times in the night, and every time I could barely talk. My throat was so raw I couldn't get my voice back. I know it must be scary for her, but she didn't let on. Tough kid.

I wondered if I would see her again. I knew that if I wanted to see her and the grandkid again, I had to try to fight this. I had an appointment with the oncologist at the end of the week, and I decided to explore the options. Just then the phone rang.

"Mr. Joey? Is that you?"

"Yeah," I answered. "Who's this, Wanda? How are ya, hon?"

"I'm good, sir. How are ya feelin' these days?" Wanda asked. "I haven't seen you, so I wanted to check in on ya. Is that okay?

"What do you think? Of course it's okay. Call me anytime, *capisce?*"

"Oh, thank you, Mr. Joey," she went on. "I actually have some interestin' news for you, my dear. You have been chosen to be *archived* in a journal ."

"Say what?"

"Well, sir, from time to time a woman features different patients and records their stories for our hospital journals," she explained. "I guess our floor was chosen to be profiled this time, and she asked if I knew someone who would make an interesting subject. I immediately thought of you."

"Wanda, I'm touched. That's really nice and all, but I don't know. I feel kind of funny tellin' a complete stranger all my business."

"You told *me*," she retorted.

"Yes, but I got to know you, rather intimately I might add, with all your pokin' and proddin'," I said half-jokingly.

"Oh my, yes, but you'll get to know this girl, too. She's a real sweetie. Besides, she does the interviews over the phone. That's much less awkward than in person," she said convincingly.

"We'll see," I said, trying to put her off.

"I kind of have to give her an answer right away, otherwise she'll move on to the next person. Did I mention she used to live near Arthur Avenue?"

"You're shittin' me!"

I finally got excited about talking to this girl. I loved talking to people from the old neighborhood.

"Count me in, Wanda!" I told her.

"Great, Mr. Joey," she said. "Don't be surprised if you get a call from her as soon as today. Oh, and please keep me posted about your treatment. After all, I miss you around here."

"No problem, Wanda. I'll let you know. Thanks for the call."

It was kind of unbelievable that I would have to share my stories with a person I had never met. But it was pretty cool that someone wanted to listen to my sick and dyin' ass. Well, I would give her the basics—and if it seemed like she had a strong constitution, she'd get the good stuff.

CHAPTER 15

"HELLO THERE, THIS IS MARIA Rossi. I'm calling for Joey Martino," the girl on the line said.

"Yeah, this is him," I answered. "What can I do you for?"

"Well, Mr. Martino, Ms. DuBois said that you gave permission for me to call and talk to you about, quite frankly, you."

"Well, that is the one subject I'm an expert on," I said smugly. "But seriously, you really find this stuff interesting? Doesn't writing about other people get monotonous?"

"Not really. I rather enjoy it," she answered. "I wouldn't do it if I weren't interested. That's important for you to know, because I really want you to be genuine and open up."

"How old are you?" I asked. "You sound like a kid."

"I'm in my thirties, and I can assure you, I've seen a lot, especially as a journalist and because of where I'm from."

"Oh yeah, you're from my neck of the woods. I haven't been over there in a while, you know, with my health and all, but before all this, I lived near the Bronx Zoo off Southern Boulevard."

And just like that, I started reminiscing, as if I were talking to an old friend about the neighborhood.

"Yeah," I said, "I used to take the D to get to Fordham. I took lots of gals to the New York Botanical Garden. You know, to smell the flowers and stuff like that."

"Sure you did," she said playfully. "I used to date a guy who went to Fordham University," Maria said.

"Oh, and the bakeries over there, mah-doan!" I got excited just thinking about them. "I love Madonia Brothers Bakery—could get a cannoli there any time of the day and it would hit the spot. Besides that, the delis over there were by far the best, and I've been all over. I remember making two, tree—heck, daily—trips into the deli, especially when I was a kid. I'd get one whiff, and I had to get a sandwich to eat on the way home."

I told her how, almost immediately the sawdust-like powder on the floor from all the Italian bread would get all over the underneath of my shoes. One time, I got cute and tried to slide through the store, and I knocked into a couple people on the line who were waiting for their numbers to be called. The guy behind the counter had come around to the front and almost smacked me upside the head. Yeah, that place always made me feel at home. All the sausage hanging from the ceiling and the fresh smells of finocchio made me want to go home and get a pot of sauce going.

"My favorite thing was the *sopressata*. I'd get a couple of slices, so thin you could almost see through it, and munch on that while I'd wait for my order. You know what I mean? You there, Maria?"

"Oh, yes, Mr. Martino," she answered attentively. "This is all great stuff. I'm writing everything down. Taking notes, if you will."

"Hey, first of all, cut the formal crap with me and call me Joey," I told her. "Second of all, why would you be writing that shit down?"

"Are you kidding me? This is not only your life, Joey, this is history and heritage," she exclaimed. "This is why I do this in the first place. I love learning about the past and things people experienced. Each of our experiences is unique, and yet sometimes you find a lot of them seem similar, relatable. It's what ties us together. It fascinates me."

"I guess I see that."

"By you explaining this to me, I felt like I was there," she said. "I could smell the bread, I could almost taste the *sopressata*. And it also takes me back to similar times in my life. I think I'm really going to enjoy this assignment."

"So, ugh, excuse me." I had to cough, and I hoped it wouldn't turn into a hack-fest. "Sorry 'bout that."

"I understand," Maria said kindly.

"How often we gonna do this, and what are you lookin' to know, in general? You know, I wanna be somewhat prepared when you call. Get my thoughts together, that kind of shi— stuff."

"Listen, Joey, if you want me to be relaxed with you, you also have to be relaxed with me," Maria said. "Don't try to clean up your act for me. Say it like it is, how you would normally talk. You know, your everyday speech."

"Whew, that's a relief, 'cause once I get going, the shit just comes flyin' out my mouth," I told her.

"Well, I guess if I could call you every weekday for about forty-five minutes, if you're up to it, we can get done in the next two weeks. I also would like to know about things from your teenage years, your profession, your home life, things like that. Wanda told me you were married a couple of times and that you have a daughter?"

"Yeah, that's right," I answered. "I got a daughter, and I think you'd like her. I'll tell ya about her. I was also in the service. What would you like to hear about next?"

"Probably your younger years," she said.

"How I got my infamous start, huh?" I laughed. "Good, I'll start with that next time you call."

We said goodbye.

Well, that was pretty painless, I said to myself. I had kinda enjoyed conjuring up old sights and sounds of my past and my old neighborhood. It was pretty cool.

The next day we spoke again, just like she said we should. I told her about my childhood, my brother James—Jay for short—and sister Joanne. I gave her all the particulars and the who's who of my family. I told her what I could remember about the spitfire I was as a child, the mischief I got into. I told her how I used to pit my sister against my brother all the time and get them into fights.

"I learned early on that I could use this as a diversion to sneak out of the house," I explained.

"Wow, so shrewd, even back then," Maria answered.

"They were both younger than me, so I always felt they had the need to outdo each other to impress me, the older brother. It was really too easy to get them goin'. But Jay, like every middle child, had a relentless need for attention, and he got noticed by excelling as a musician."

"That's great."

We spoke a lot about my teenage years—yes, I was a punk, and yes, I smoked by the age of twelve, and oh well. She wanted to know more about Jay and where he was now.

"Well dear, Jay is a case of wasted talent. De Niro described this term best in *A Bronx Tale*. It was a catchphrase from the movie. You know, to have such talent and potential, only to get caught up with the wrong things and waste it. I guess you could say, maybe we all do that to some extent," I said with lament. "We had high hopes for him. Jay was talented but weak."

"How do you mean?"

"He was on his way to the top," I said, feeling my voice getting angry. "He was part of a band, big recording contract and the whole nine. Did concerts up the ying-yang. But it was the seventies and he got caught up in the shit, ya know, coke. Anyway, long story short, that was the end of that. What ya gonna do?"

"What does that mean?" she asked.

"What do you mean, 'what does that mean?'"

I thought my summary was quite clear. In addition my brother was sort of famous, so I didn't want to get into too many sordid details.

"Listen, sweetheart," I told her, "he was a big name in the rock scene. You probably wouldn't know him, because his music was a little before your time. But his life didn't turn out glamorous, my friend. He's in jail."

"Oh my. How long has it been?" Maria asked.

"It's been a while. He's due to get out soon, again."

"Ah, so this is a recurring thing with him?"

"Yeah, but more like a recurring nightmare for my family," I explained. "Mah-doan, my poor mother's heartache for her son—and my father, fuhgeddaboutit. He wanted to rip Jay's head off so many times, and he came close, too. You see, Jay's band is still somewhat together, but he was replaced several times because of his drug problem. It got in the way of everything. And do you know at one time he was called one of the greats of the guitar world? Man, it really pisses me off. He had so many chances and fucked it up so many times. He just lived the high life, literally, and thought he could turn it off whenever he wanted to."

She wanted to know more.

"Did he ever have any kids?"

"Yeah, two yuppie shitheads who bleed him dry, even now, even though he has nothin'," I said. "You see, he's in jail for tax evasion, not actually getting caught *using*. He had a problem and desperately needed professional help. This was before all the rehab shit you hear about now.

He tried to get clean many times, but had no support. His wife was right along with him in the beginning. She managed to straighten up for a time when the kids came along. Shortly after, she turned her sights on pills, and that was no picnic, certainly no help for Jay.

"Look, just about everyone did drugs back then. I was certainly no choirboy myself, but he was so out of control that he was out of the band more than he was in. Eventually, he was out for good and got involved with techie stuff, computers. He was good at that too, but I guess he also made money from his drug involvement, if you know what I mean. Anyway, years later the government caught up with him. You know how that goes."

"No, I don't, explain it to me," Maria said flatly.

"C'mon, I thought you were a smart kid," I told her. "Don't you know that the government couldn't give two shits if you're destroyin' yourself with drugs? If they did, there'd be more rehab services for those poor bastards in jail for usin' the shit. The government doesn't concern itself with large penalties for that, because then you can be in and out of the system. Eventually, you're asked to be a snitch and give up the dealer—and that's who gets the big penalties.

"The government can't stand getting ripped off, and in their eyes that's what drug dealers do. It's money under the table that doesn't get taxed, and to them that's a bigger crime than even some murders. After all, the illegal drug dealers are only steppin' on the toes of the legal ones. Pharmaceuticals are where it's at, and big gov makes a lotta money on that. Hell, they make a ton just off me! You should see my dining table. It's full of prescription drugs that I need to take daily, and that's not including anything for the cancer that's killin' me."

"You're obviously pretty opinionated about the subject," Maria said. "I'm sure government officials wouldn't see it that way."

"I'm sure not. Hey, you tryin' to get me on a roll today?"

"Yeah, I guess I just wanted to get your thoughts and feelings out about your brother. I wasn't expecting all this of course."

"It's just a sad state of affairs. It's a shame, a damn shame and a waste, *capisce*?

"*Capisce*," Maria answered.

I wasn't feeling well, so we cut things short. The day after that she asked me about my time in the service. This conversation was even more upsetting than the previous day.

CHAPTER 16

"WHAT DO YA WANT TO know?" I asked. "My time in the service is pretty boring stuff."

"Let me be the judge of that."

"Well, I was in from 1961 to '65, airman first class in the United States Air Force," I began. "I was stationed at McGuire Air Force Base, and I was a mechanic for most of my time."

"Wow, were you involved in Vietnam?" she asked.

"Not really," I answered sheepishly. "I got out just in time. The Vietnam War officially started in 1964. Our first combat troops arrived there the year I got out, but it had been building up for years before."

There was an awkward pause. "You say that as if you had known it was coming."

I shifted my position on the chair and thought for a minute before answering. It seemed necessary to give her a slight education without revealing too much personal information.

"Well, the U.S. was 'involved' since '61. This is before your time, and I don't know how much you know about what happened, but if you're like most people, you know many people here did not support the war. It was a tragedy for us and a huge blemish on our history."

"I do know that Vietnam, or the Vietnam War, was really a conflict between North Vietnam and South Vietnam, and each had their own allies around the world, and it went on for the better part of a decade," she answered.

"Okay, so I can tell you do know a few more facts than most," I chuckled and then coughed. I still couldn't seem to laugh without coughing. "How did you get so smart?"

"I am a journalist, remember," she answered. "I have to know a little about a lot."

"Well, you are right," I started. "And I'm sure you know North Vietnam was aligned with the Soviet Union and China, while South Vietnam had its allies, most notably the U.S."

She answered affirmatively.

"For the U.S., our start date was probably 1961," I went on. "We sent advisors over there in the '50s. We had some battalions on patrol there in '61, along with helicopters and air and ground crewmen. Later, we sent naval vessels. You have to remember, there was fighting there for a long time before we ever got there, since 1945. The situation just kept escalating."

"Were you ever privy to what was happening over there as things were unfolding?" Maria asked.

"Well, some of our pilots got to train and fly support missions over there in the South," I explained. "This was in '61, when I was a rookie, so to speak. I tested high for knowledge of the planes. I actually worked as a mechanic on some planes that went over there. So yeah, I had some knowledge of aircraft and when they were going over. I got my basic training in air traffic control while I was at the base, and I really loved that. I was even sent over to Germany for a while toward the end of my run. My time was good with the air force ... but bad personally."

"Why? What happened?"

"I met somebody." Looking down at the floor, I told her it was pretty intense.

"Do you want to talk about it?" Maria asked.

"Sure, why not," I told her. "It was a wild time, you know, an experimental time for all of us back then."

"How so?"

"Drugs ... paraphernalia, psychedelics, things like that,"

I thought, *This girl is too green for me to get into the nitty-gritty about drugs.* I could tell that even over the phone. Plus, I didn't want to corrupt her mind.

"So while I was in Germany, I got chummy with some guys in my barracks. Two were Italian, two Irish, and one black guy. All were from either New York, New Jersey, or Philly—you know, we could all relate. One of the guys had a friend named Peter from Munich who would let us drive him around and pay his bar tab in exchange for the use of his car and smokes. It worked out great. He'd be in the bar drinkin' like a fuckin' fish, gettin' piss drunk with some of the guys, while one of us, sometimes two at a time, would take girls in the car for a little bada-boom, *capisce*?"

"Yeah, yeah, I get it. Continue," she commanded.

"Most of the time these were just girls we met at the bar. Then one day, Peter brought along his sister and some of her friends. I guess she was bustin' his chops about wanting to meet service guys. I remember, he told us all specifically we could have at any of the girls, but his sister Sharon was off-limits."

"Uh oh. I can already tell where this is going," Maria interrupted.

"You have to understand, I was a handsome devil back then," I chuckled. "I had a wild personality to boot. I used to get in fights, and I was always tellin' jokes and cuttin' up. Most of the time, girls just came up to me. I guess they just liked what they saw. What can I say?"

"So did you wind up going with Sharon?"

I paused, because as I was retelling the story, I thought about the irony of life. It's weird how things play out. One set of circumstances affects another; it's like a chain reaction in the universe.

"I didn't at first," I continued. "She gave me eyes the minute she sat at the bar. I thought she was gorgeous. Blonde hair, hazel eyes, dimples, and this little gap between her two front teeth, like Lauren Hutton. I thought that was sexy. She smoked and had a little bit of a raspy voice. And her body was out of sight. Nice cans too, pardon the expression. I had all I could do to keep away from her.

"I diverted my attention by making time with one of her friends. That was a mistake. The friend started liking me, and now Sharon was upset with the friend and she pulled an attitude with me. After a while it turned into a big mess. Anyway, I guess they both realized it would be better for their friendship if they both stayed away from me. Then I went from being 'most wanted' to a leper." I shook my head, remembering.

"Then one night, this guy Peter wanted to go out, and some of the other guys had the flu. So me and Lou from Philly were going to go with him. Unbeknownst to me, Peter brought Sharon. So when they picked us up at the meeting spot, there was complete silence on the way to the bar.

"Now, Lou and Peter and I were having a raucous time drinkin' and hangin' out at the bar, and even though Sharon could hold her own with the drinks, she looked kinda sad. So I started talkin' to her. Boy, did we have a great conversation. She knew so much about what was goin' on in the world and was so interested in the work we were doing in the military. She was compassionate, and funny. Did I mention she had a filthy mouth like me?"

"She sounds terrific," Maria said.

"Yeah, but you know, I'da felt like a real strunze if I made a move. That's the cardinal rule between guys. You don't fuck around when it comes to their sisters or wives—unless, of course, you have their blessing. Which is what ended up happening, probably—no, most definitely—because I saved his ass one night.

"Peter loved me. He thought I was a riot. But this one night some mammaluke decided to poke holes in Peter's tires. Who knows why? Maybe because he saw Peter with American servicemen, or maybe because we were havin' too good of a time. Who the fuck knows? Anyway, we saw the guy runnin' away. Nothing we could do. So Lou and me footed the bill and got Peter new tires. Basically, that cost us everything we would have gotten paid that month. We were all pissed but Peter took it harder than us. For the next couple of nights out, Peter just wanted to hang at that one bar, never wanted to leave, always the same bar. So one night, all of us guys were together and Peter went to take a piss. After he was gone a while I said to myself, *What did he do, go to China to take a piss?*"

"Where was he?" Maria asked.

"Well, that's when I looked over, and who did I see getting the shit knocked out of him? Peter! I yelled out to the guys and then jumped on the guy throwin' the punches. It was the guy who had slashed the tires. By instinct, I grabbed him by the neck and threw him up against the bar. I beat him upside the head pretty good, until we all got thrown out.

"The guys and me didn't want any trouble, so we left. But we waited for the asshole, and when he set foot out of the bar, we threw a blanket we had in the car over him and had ourselves a little blanket party. That way he would at least be recognizable. You know, I do have a heart. We took turns punchin' and kickin' the shit out of this guy until he begged for mercy. Stupid ass. Anyway, after that incident, Peter felt vindicated and in debt to me. He had no beef with me askin' Sharon out on a date. And that's just what I did."

"Well, that's some story," Maria said. "And look how it worked out in your favor. Good for you."

"I guess." I stopped and took a drag on my cigarette. I felt I needed one at this point. Reliving this time in my life was bittersweet.

"Are you smoking?" Maria's voice was shocked.

"And whadda you care?" I asked. "Are you being asked to talk about difficult times in your life? You don't know what's going through my mind. You shouldn't be judging me, kid."

"Oh, I'm not judging your story or you," she answered. "I'm just concerned for your well-being. And I'm a little thrown by it, too. I'm sorry."

"Well-being!" I exclaimed. "Ha, what well-being? You gotta be kiddin' me. I'm dying, sweetheart. My wellness stopped a long time ago. I'll smoke if I want to."

"I see," she said coldly.

It seemed as if she got emotional for a minute and then regained her equilibrium as an unbiased journalist. Funny what triggered emotion in people: the retelling of a story from a nostalgic time, the fact that a man dying of cancer had the balls to still smoke cigarettes. It is what it is.

"Let's continue," Maria urged. "I want to find out why *this* particular story sparks so much fire in you. Was it difficult because of the conditions in the world at that time?"

"Not so much," I answered as I put my cigarette butt out. "Remember, things got worse with the war, after I got out. Before that, the situation with Sharon got more intense, ya know."

"No, I don't know."

I could tell Maria wanted the full story.

"We fell in love." I finally spit it out. "I think it was my first time ever being truly in love."

"Really?"

"Yeah." I figured I might as well tell her the whole story. "The next night after the fight, we all found ourselves back at the scene of the crime. The bar was jumpin'. Sharon was there with her friends.

The whole night I just felt weird. The minute Peter told me I had the green light, I had knots in my stomach. The excitement went through my veins. That anticipation of knowing what I was about to do had me amped up all night. We were all up dancing. 'I Got You Babe' was playin', and we all broke into song, kinda like karaoke today. We were drinkin' and hammin' it up."

I told Maria the rest of it. When the song was over, everyone had deserted the dance floor, probably for drink refills. Then "Georgia on My Mind" by Ray Charles started playing, and my eyes met Sharon's. My heart was racing, but I had to play it cool. I gave her a nod and put out my hand to her. She grabbed it, and I led her to a little table in the corner. I gently sat her on the table, and I leaned in. I told her, "You know what this song is gonna remind me of every time I hear it from now on, no matter where I'm at?" She looked at me coyly, and I said, "Your beautiful face." And with that, I leaned in for the kiss, and it was all over.

It seemed to last forever. It felt like we were the only two people there. I wanted to freeze that feeling, that moment. I told her I was falling.

"And you know what she said back?" I asked Maria

"What did she say?" Maria answered eagerly.

"She said, 'I've been falling. I've just been waiting for you to catch me.' So I told her, 'Consider yourself caught.' It was too good to be true."

"Wow, it sounds like a movie," Maria swooned.

"I know, and that's how we continued for quite some time. She really pampered me when I was with her. She cooked for me. We went camping a lot when I was on breaks. We had sex every chance we got. It was the best when we were camping, though, under the stars, no one around. She took me to a lot of places, too. I saw Europe because of her. Sometimes everyone would join in on our camping trips, and that was a lot of fun. Peter was always good for the provisions, if you know what I mean."

"Like what—alcohol, pot?" Maria asked.

"Oh yeah, weed was never a problem. We were in Amsterdam a lot. But Peter liked to push the envelope when it came to drugs and was always bringing experimental shit. He was obsessed with Timothy Leary and all the research goin' on at that time with psychedelics. He brought us stuff like magic mushrooms, opiates, and all kinds of shit. We tried it all. We had nothin' to lose. Besides, we had nobody to answer to when we were out camping. For me, I was with my girl under the stars, and life couldn't get any better then."

"Did you guys ever discuss your return to the U.S.?" Maria asked.

"It came up a couple of times, but I tried to avoid it. I'm not a planner, and I didn't want to think that far ahead. I loved being in love, and I didn't want it to end. To tell you the truth, I wanted to stay there. I didn't want to go back to the States after I met her."

"So what happened, did you get your heart broken? Did she break up with you?" Maria was eager to know.

"She broke my heart all right, but she didn't break up with me." I had to light up again. "Sorry, gotta have another smoke. You don't mind, do ya?"

"Hey, it's your life,"

"It certainly is." I took a deep drag. "Listen, one night before I had to head back to the States we were camping, lying under the stars and having a heart-to-heart. Her hand was in mine, and I told her I loved her. I meant it too. I was contemplating finishing up my duty at home and either sending for her or heading right back to Germany to be with her. There was something so intriguing about her. She had a passion for life. I just knew I loved being with her and around her.

"Everyone was out there with us that night, but we were off by ourselves in our own little world. There was a bonfire, and we decided to join in. There were people there who I had never met before. You know how it is when you're young and hangin' out, everybody knows somebody, and one person tells another and another, and before you know it, you're havin' yourself a party. So drugs were everywhere. Every person there was doing something."

"Sounds like a wild time," Maria said.

"You better believe it. Some people were hallucinating and shit. It got crazy. Pipes were being passed around; people were licking square papers, not even knowing what they were doing. Plus we were all drinkin'. It was totally not a scene for a novice. Sharon and I were just glued to each other, takin' it all in. We used to smoke and do drugs together, and we agreed it heightened our experiences. She was used to the drug scene, but when she was with me I think she tried more because I could monitor her, and I pretty much always had it together.

"But then her girlfriends got ahold of her, and they decided to do 'shrooms. I was hangin' with the boys for a while, and she wandered back my way sometime later. She immediately started hangin' on me and beggin' me to try the shit she was on. I told her to calm down. 'Later, later,' I told her, but she wouldn't let up. She was totally trippin' by then and wanted me to join her. She started gettin' anxious and agitated. She was scratchin' her skin a lot, and I knew somethin' wasn't right. She was havin' a bad trip. I gave her water and made her lie down in the tent. She started complainin' of being really cold, and she was shiverin' and shakin'. Before I knew it, her body was out of control, and I told her friend to go get Peter. I was gonna have him give me the car so I could get her to a hospital if she got worse."

"So what happened? Was it a bad trip," Maria asked.

"Yeah …" I trailed off.

"Joey … are you still there?"

I almost couldn't hear Maria. I could barely make my mouth move. It was a minute before I could utter a word.

"She died," I whispered.

"What?" Maria exclaimed. "Oh my gosh, Joey, how horrible."

There was silence again as I reflected on the enormity of what had happened.

"She had a seizure; she died in my arms," I finally said. "Peter was there, her friends were there. They all watched in horror as I suddenly started breathin' into her mouth and beating on her chest after she was gone. I knew CPR, and I just snapped. It was like in an instant I became an animal. I was all over her, so focused on reviving her. I thought I could still save her. I was squeezing her hand, yellin' at her to open her eyes. I was huggin' her and rockin' her and even pinchin' her skin to see if I could get some reaction or sign of life.

"But hope was gone. I just didn't wanna face it. Peter was tryin' to get me off her and restrain me. Meanwhile, he started spewin' off at the mouth at the girls, demandin' they tell him what they gave her. They were all sobbing uncontrollably except one girl, the girl I got together with. She was sittin' off to the side with her mouth hangin' open, just staring at Sharon. She told us they all did 'shrooms together. I later found out Sharon had had seizures in the past, but this was definitely a bad trip. It triggered a seizure in her, and her heart just stopped. Just like that."

I had to pause for a minute.

"I couldn't believe it. *How could this be*, I thought to myself over and over. I couldn't face my loss, but the loss of her life period. She was a beautiful, smart and special girl whom countless people would never get to meet. She had a bright future, and in an instant it was snatched. And for what—a moment of pleasure, or at least what we thought was pleasure? She was gone, just like that. What a waste.

"The coroner said it was a heart attack, and none of us was ever implicated. But at the time I didn't care either way. I felt responsible for looking after her, and I had failed. She was my girl, she was with me. I knew I never wanted to feel responsible for anyone ever again. I felt like my life was over. My ability to love sure was."

CHAPTER 17

I HAD BEEN HALF RIGHT, thinking I would bore Maria to tears, telling her about my time in the military. She wasn't bored, but she was in tears all right. She was downright sobbin' by the time I was done with my story. I definitely didn't want to relive that time, but we had headed down that pathway, and next thing I knew I was talking about it.

I couldn't believe I was actually saying those things out loud. I'd replayed that awful night and thought about it and Sharon so many times, but I'd never really talked about it. It kind of felt good to share it now.

I liked this Maria. She was easy to talk to. Next time she called I was gonna try to cheer her up with some funny shit.

My phone rang, and it was Nina. A morning call was out of character for her.

"Hello, Dad," she said cheerfully. "How are you feeling?"

"So-so." My voice was so raspy in the morning. I probably sounded terrible to her.

"How's it going? What have your days been like?"

"Oh, they're pretty routine now," I answered. "Charo gets me up in the morning and makes coffee. On a good day when I'm not coughing up a lung, I have a couple of cigs and a quick read through the paper. I take my pills, and by then I'm exhausted. But that Charo is a pisser, and she makes sure I take my shower. She helps me do what I gotta do. By then I'm usually so worn out I just go back to bed until lunch, and sometimes I even sleep through that. Until Maria calls."

"Who's Maria?" Nina asked. "You have another daughter I don't know about?"

"Very funny, wiseass," I kidded back. "Fuckin' forgot to tell you about her. I tell ya, the mind is going, Nina. She's this young girl who's profiling me for the hospital journals. She's interviewing me about my life, and man are we getting into some shit. She's from my neck of the woods, so we can relate to each other despite the big generation gap. But she's smart and knows about stuff most people her age don't even give a shit about."

"Like what?" Nina asked.

"Well, so far we've discussed Vietnam, the old neighborhood, you know—things. Every time we talk, it's a new topic. I think she reads a lot. She reminds me of you."

"Really? Gee I thought I was unique." There was a hint of jealousy in her voice.

"Never mind. So, to what do I owe the honor of a morning call?"

"Well it's a special day in my house today," Nina said. "It's somebody's birthday."

"Well I know it's not yours, so it must be the little man's."

"You got it!" she said gleefully.

I could tell she lit up with a smile every time she talked about him.

"He's turning one, so this is a big day. Would you like to wish him a happy birthday?"

"Of course, of course," I played along.

I could hear her talking to him in a babyish voice, and before I knew it, he was giggling and shouting into the phone.

"Happy birthday, young man!" I said. "You're getting to be a big boy. Gonna be shavin' soon, pal." I chuckled.

Then I started coughing. Jack laughed and started causing a ruckus back at me through the phone. I think he thought I was playing.

Nina got back on the phone.

"What's going on, you all right?"

"Yeah, yeah, you know how it is." I tried to play it off. "That boy is a pisser. He's feisty. Every time I'd cough, he yelled back at me. We were communicatin'."

"Well, you've got to take in a lot of warm fluids I think, other than coffee—more like chicken soup. Does Charo cook?"

"Yeah, yeah, Charo will do whatever I ask her to do. I'm not in the chicken soup kind of mood," I told her. "It is what it is, what ya gonna do."

"Well what *are* you going to do?" she asked. "Are you going to try any other treatments? Have you given any thought to what's next?"

"Sure I have," I answered indignantly. She talked to me like I was a child lately. "I don't know if I wanna be a guinea pig again. It was torture, and I don't know if I wanna put myself through that again if the outcome is gonna be the same anyway."

"But you won't know any of that unless you try," she reasoned. "You may be able to take something that won't make you feel so ill." Her voice was pleading.

"We'll see."

Funny, I remembered when she was a kid, I used to say "We'll see" as a way of saying no without hurting her feelings.

"Radiation might be an option," I told her. "I'll talk it over with the doc at my appointment this week. Does that make you feel better?"

"Don't do it to make me feel better. After everything and all our talks—do it to *get* better for yourself and your family."

"I hear what you're sayin', but do you realize that I'm not gonna get better?" I snapped. "It's stage four. I'd only be prolonging the inevitable."

"Is that how you really feel? Because I remember a conversation when you were gasping for breath, trying to get into bed and get warm. You were dreaming and talking about your life and coming to Florida one day."

"That would be nice," I agreed. "I'm afraid it might only be a dream. Like I said, let's wait and see what the doc says this week."

Uh oh. I felt another round of coughing coming on. "Listen, I gotta go. Give the kid a hug for me. I love ya."

I know she was only looking out for me, but it was a waste of time. I hated to tell her that.

I slept the rest of that morning away, interrupted only by bouts of coughing. Then Maria called, a little later than usual, and I had to gather my thoughts.

"Maria, how you doin', hon?" I asked her.

"Well, if you must know, I'm still a little shaken from your story yesterday," she answered. "I gotta tell you, I didn't really expect the outcome. Your heart getting broken was hard enough to believe."

"What, you don't think of me as a romantic who's had his heart broken once or twice?" I asked playfully.

I tried to lighten the mood because I really didn't want to revisit Sharon's death.

"Not so much, no," Maria answered.

We chuckled, and then she got right into it. She wanted to know what I did for work when I got back home. I explained that I had taken a job as a mechanic at a trucking company before finally landing my dream job working as an air traffic controller.

Then she wanted to know how I met my ex-wife, Caroline. This kid must have thought I was some kind of killer Casanova, because she never seemed to believe that I was capable of falling in love. Don't know how she could assume that about me just over the phone, unless she was simply bitter toward all men in general.

"I get the sense that you can't believe I was actually married," I asked her.

"Well, for one thing you seem so tough and rugged, not exactly a guy who falls in love easily," she explained. "And I guess after your story about Sharon, I would have thought it would be a long time before you found someone as special as her—special enough to marry."

"You're right on both counts," I told her. "I am a tough guy. And it was a long time before I *thought* anyone was as special as Sharon. I think that was part of my problem for a long time, even with my wife. I never thought anyone would measure up to that first intense love I had with Sharon."

"So were you searching?"

"I was searchin' everywhere … but for something I already had, especially while I was married. I came to realize that only after it was too late. Especially now that I see what a great person my daughter turned out to be. I realize that is because of Caroline. She was a gem."

"So what brought you two together?" Maria asked.

"Her brother."

"Another-fix up by the brother?" she questioned. "Weren't you ambivalent?"

"I guess you would think so, but this was totally different," I explained.

"I met her brother Vinnie at the trucking company. He was a real regular guy and funny as shit. We had similar family situations—both from the Bronx, both Italian, and we both had a brother and sister. We could relate to each other. So we used to get off work and grab a beer with a few other guys. One day Vinnie asked me to look at his car. It was actin' up so I told him I would keep it at my house and fix it. That's how I made some side money. So I had to drop him off at his house. That's when I saw her on the stoop."

"Sounds like the same scenario to me," Maria interjected.

"I could see how you might think that, but trust me, these were two totally different type of broads we're talkin' about here. So I saw Caroline, and she had jet-black hair, big, green eyes, and a smile as wide as the Pacific. She was really skinny, frail-lookin', and petite. It was that smile and those kind eyes that drew me in."

"Seems like you thought she was pretty," Maria observed. "Were you right about her? Was she kind?"

"Oh yeah. Not a hard woman at all. Very sweet and kinda shy. She had the softest voice when she told me her name was Caroline. Not the kinda girl I ever really messed with." I pondered this as the words were coming out of my mouth.

"So what made you pursue her?" Maria asked. "I mean, after all, she was your new friend's sister, and you had that cardinal rule."

"Yeah, yeah, don't get cute," I said. "When I saw her on the stoop that day, I was hot and sweaty, and she offered me some lemonade. Summers are murder here, as you know. I had just gotten through working, and I was all greasy and grimy. So I took her up on the offer, and we sat on her porch makin' small talk while Vinnie went up to take a shower. Well, when he was done he came outside and chimed in with us. We all talked, and he didn't seem to mind one bit that I was takin' up with her. But it was all friendly. They were both just genuinely nice. Good people."

"Does that mean you were all friends for a while?"

"Sort of. Caroline and I usually made small talk when we ran into each other after that. Like I said, I thought she was pretty, but I figured she was out of my league, to tell you the truth. I never really thought about pursuing it."

"So how did it happen?" Maria asked.

"How did what happen?"

"You know, your first date, your first kiss. What finally got you two together?"

"Well, right after that first meeting on the porch, Vinnie told me that his sister thought I was really cute. He suggested I take her out, but then he warned me to be on my best behavior, otherwise I'd hear it from his father. At that time I wasn't lookin' for anything serious. I knew if I dated Caroline I would really have to give it my all. She was respectable. She was the marrying kind, if you know what I mean."

"Yeah, I get it. Go on."

"Well, I knew I had the green light. So after a couple of weeks went by, I got up the nerve to ask her out. She said yes, but I would have to ask her father's permission and tell her father and mother our plans. They told me exactly what time to have her back. You have to understand, this wasn't unusual for those days, but *I* wasn't used to it. But since I really wanted to take Caroline on a date, I did it. I took her for pizza and to an ice cream parlor."

"So how did it go? Did you try to kiss her when it was over? Did you have her back on time?"

"A, oh! What's with the third degree about the date?"

"Hey, I'm just doing my job," Maria defended herself. "Anyway, this is the good stuff, and this *is* the woman you married and had a child with. So, heck yeah I want to know the juice."

"We had a great time talkin'," I explained. "We kept it light. She wasn't into politics and didn't know much about world events, but she seemed very interested about me. She asked a lot of questions, and we compared notes. She was very sweet. But to answer your other two questions: I had her back just in time, and no, I didn't try to kiss her. Even though I wasn't used to girls like her, I certainly knew the rules. And you didn't even try to get a kiss on the first date unless you wanted to get slapped."

"Good for you!"

"On the date I found out I knew a couple girls she went to high school with. Now, *they* were easy to get a kiss from. We actually laughed about that," I revealed. "Caroline sure was pretty. She looked like young Liz Taylor, maybe Joan Collins. A real beauty, and I felt ten feet tall with her on my arm."

"So how did you get to the next level with Caroline?" Maria wanted to know.

"Quite frankly, things took time, even though I knew she was into me," I said.

I didn't know how to be delicate about the next subject. "She was … um … pure, so lots of things were on hold … if you know what I mean."

"She was a virgin?"

"Um, yeah," I said awkwardly. "She wanted to go steady, which we did, but before I said yes to that, I almost had to know in my mind that I would marry her. I felt otherwise, why waste my time? When I first dated her, although I really liked her and she made me feel so special, a guy still has needs … know what I'm sayin'?"

"So you're saying you dated other girls for those … needs … in the beginning, correct?" Maria interrogated.

"You got it!" I agreed.

I still didn't think Maria realized how green Caroline was back then, as were lots of girls in those days.

"Maria, you have to understand that the birds and the bees were not really explained in many households back then. However, it was a new generation, a new time in the world, and many women were figurin' things out on their own and tellin' friends about what they were learning. Some information was accurate, but some was not. Somewhere along the line Caroline got her share of wrong info. She was a bit of an extreme case, though."

"How so?" Maria seemed interested.

"I'll give you a scenario to help you understand," I started. "She told me this story. One night when she was a senior in high school, she went on a date to a drive-in movie. She was a little resistant while she and the boy kissed, and she had her arm in between herself and the guy the whole time. He wound up giving her a hickey, by accident, of course."

"Oh sure," Maria interrupted sarcastically.

I got the vibe that Maria knew the way guys were.

"Anyway, she didn't realize it until the next day. She covered it up by wearin' a turtleneck to school. Come to find out, she thought her life was over. She was depressed and spent the whole day cryin', until one of her friends consoled her as they walked home from school. Caroline finally told her friend why she was upset; she thought she was pregnant, because of the hickey! Caroline told me her friend hugged her, told her everything was all right, and then laughed so hard you could hear her a mile away. Then her friend explained sex—only from what she had *heard*, of course. They both had a good laugh, but needless to say, Caroline was a little embarrassed."

"Wow, was she naïve! I can't believe she actually told you that," Maria said in amazement. "That took guts."

"How do you mean?" I asked.

"Well, Caroline must have really had confidence that you wouldn't laugh at her upon hearing a story like that."

"Gee, I never really looked at it that way at the time, but you might be right." I thought about it for a few seconds. "For a young kid, you sure have some good insights into shit."

"Thanks, I think," she answered. "So what *did* you do when she told you?"

"I did laugh a little, but *with* her, not *at* her. I told her it was cute, and that her innocence was attractive to me. I don't think I made her feel silly in any way. So that's why, when *I* gave her a hickey, I took responsibility. I told her how to try and get rid of it. I told her to comb it out and put that makeup stuff you girls wear on your face over it. She opted for a turtleneck again."

"That's funny," Maria chuckled. "So how long were you were an official couple?"

"We dated for a little over a year before I popped the question. Of course, I asked the father first. I got the blessing, but I also got the third degree."

"How so?"

"Well, I don't think her parents were convinced I was ready for marriage," I replied. "And they definitely didn't think I was good enough for their daughter. They pretty much told me that. They even went with me to pick out the ring. I did the best I could for a twenty-four-year-old guy. What ya gonna do?"

"So you got married. And when did the baby come along?"

"Well, hold up." I halted her questioning. "Caroline and I did our fair share of breaking up and making up. Unfortunately, our biggest break-up was right before the wedding."

"What do you mean, *right before the wedding*? How close are we talking?"

"About a week before."

It sounded horrible to say. God only knew what this girl was thinking.

"Listen, I know this is probably not going to make your journal and all, but let me explain the scenario. Caroline and I had broken up before. She used to fight with me over my family. She felt they didn't like her because she wasn't a full-blooded Italian. She was part Irish, on her mother's side. She always thought my family was trying to break us up. This wasn't true.

"In addition, at twenty-one years old, she was also a little insecure and thought I had a wanderin' eye. So she had her suspicions. But truth be told, I had mine, too. She had a very handsome neighbor who used to hang with her on the stoop all the time. I was a little bothered at first, but she put my mind at ease about them just being friends. After a while, I got the feeling that he was pitchin' for the wrong team, if ya know what I mean, *capisce?*"

"You thought he could be gay?"

"Possibly, so then I stopped givin' her shit about it. Now, all the pressure of *the wedding* and actually getting married was getting to me. Sure, I was finally going to get to the Promised Land with her, but then I would have to start being a responsible guy, for her and for me. It was too much for me to deal with. So we had a blowout, and we called it off. Our families were beside themselves. Caroline was devastated."

"But obviously you worked it out somehow," Maria said brightly. "What was it that finally brought you back together?"

"We didn't want to be—"

"Oh my gosh, Joey, I hate to interrupt, but I just realized I'm late for another appointment. I'm so sorry, but I have to go. I can't wait to talk to you tomorrow."

"Okay, kid, speak to ya tomorrow."

I was going to tell her that Caroline and I didn't want to be apart. At the time, we thought we did, but when faced with actually being away from each other, we realized we had made a big mistake. Unfortunately, it was a mistake I would make again and again. I had found comfort with Caroline, yet I never seemed to know when I had it good. Instead, I was always trying to run away from anything safe and good. How screwed up was that?

It was a side of myself I hated, and I hated the thought of revealing it to Maria. But not for fear she would write about it. Hell, I was telling her stuff at this point I knew she wouldn't add to her story. I guess I was starting to like this kid, and I cared a little what she thought. The funny thing was, for most of my life I had never really cared what anyone thought of me.

CHAPTER 18

THAT NIGHT WAS TERRIBLE. I had the sweats. I was coughing unmercifully, so bad I thought I had broken my ribs. When I mustered the strength to go to the bathroom, I noticed I had broken blood vessels all over my face. I was hoping the morning would bring me some relief. I was exhausted from my sporadic fits, and when the morning finally arrived, I slumped over in a heap on top of the bed, and a gentle slumber took over my body for most of the day.

I had missed Maria's first call. Apparently, this worried her, so when she called again and I answered, she was a little animated.

"Oh, my gosh! Are you okay?" she asked in a near-shriek. "I called and you didn't answer, even though I let the phone ring dozens of times. I thought maybe something was very wrong."

"No, I'm okay," I answered, trying to find my voice. "Just had a really bad night. It happens more often than not lately. I can't believe I slept the day away, though. Wow, that was some deep sleep. I woke up and didn't even know where I was or what day it was for that matter.."

"That could be a good thing," Maria said, more calmly now. "It's Friday by the way and the end of our first week. I want to apologize about yesterday. We were at a very important turning point in your story, your life, and I hated to cut you short."

"I appreciate that."

"I've been anticipating hearing more," Maria said anxiously. "So how exactly did you rectify the situation with Caroline?"

"Well, it was no picnic in the park, I can tell ya that," I said matter-of-factly. "At first we were both pissed. Both our families were at odds with one another."

"Oh, I'm sure," Maria said. "With the wedding being cancelled, who could blame them?"

"You can only imagine how it went down," I continued. "Once the initial shock wore off, I think we were all a little bitter. Then Caroline and I started missin' each other, without the other one realizing it. I wondered if she would answer if I called. I tried it a couple of times, but everyone hung up on me. I think she was forbidden to see me or talk to me. But I found out she really wanted to."

"So what did you do?"

"I drove by her house and would wait till I saw her on the stoop. Then I'd try to approach her. I was always intercepted and told to leave—even by her brother! So one day I parked up the hill from her house. She walked most everywhere she had to go, and I waited for her on a day I knew she usually went to the grocery store. Just when I saw her, I jumped out of my car and stepped in front of her. I startled her, but she stopped and stared at me with those big, green eyes. She said, 'What are you doing here? I suppose you want your ring back.' I just held out my hand for hers and told her I wanted *her* back. She put her hand in mine and sat with me in the car, and we talked, and cried, and talked some more. We knew then and there that we were going to work this out between us. Handlin' the families was another story."

"How did they react? It must have been grueling," Maria empathized. "I had a similar situation happen to me, minus the wedding plans, and my mom was not a happy camper."

"What did your father do?" I was curious to know. How parents act during their child's triumphs and disappointments can really define the kind of person the child becomes. I felt Maria was a pretty good kid. I wondered how she got that way.

"Oh, we had to keep my father in the dark for a while until we could smooth things over," Maria admitted. "It would not have been pretty otherwise."

"You can understand my dilemma then," I said. "After watching Caroline mope around like a lovesick puppy dog and watching me act like a moody bastard, the families agreed to iron this thing out. We were able to get another date at the church and convince the caterer and manager of the social hall to make room for us—well, after I had a little, let us say, 'talk' with them. Needless to say, after that chat, it worked out fine."

"Well, that's sounds great," Maria said. "I would say happily ever after, but I know you and Caroline didn't last. Why not?"

"It's complicated."

"Was it someone else? Was it money? Was it your daughter?" Maria really wanted the dirt.

"Nah, it really wasn't any of those things." As I said that, I chuckled inside. Those were most of the things that people fought over, the things that broke them apart. At least that was what the self-help assholes told ya. So if these weren't our problems, why didn't we work out?

I had to think about the answer....

I guess I would never really be able to sum it all up. Why should I have to? I didn't know this girl from a hole in the wall. I mean, we were getting to know each other's lives, given this unique situation, but hell, I didn't even know what she looked like. If I passed her on the street, I would never know it. This girl on the other end of the phone had a bit more than a snapshot of my life already, and yet she wanted some deep questions answered. How odd that someone would care so much to know my deepest personal thoughts. My life was only to be fodder for a small publication that might never be read.

Yet when I thought about the situation, it had been a blessing in disguise. I had been able to share my story more easily with Maria *because* I didn't really know her. It had been the therapy I'd resisted all my life, now that I was at the end of my life—sort of a life in review. The shame of it all was that now that I was giving so much care and thought to all these situations, I realized I should have done so at the time they were happening. Then maybe things would have been different for me. What ya gonna do?

Meanwhile, Maria was waiting for something profound to come out of my mouth. The truth was, I had nothing concrete to give her. There was no easy answer, but I knew I had to take some ownership of the breakup of my marriage.

"Maria, it was mostly me," I started. "I know it takes two to tango, but I wasn't committed like a married man should be."

"What makes you feel it was mostly you?"

"Well, if you must know, once a bachelor, always a bachelor," I said half-heartedly. "What can I say, I loved the single life. I loved to go out after work with my buddies and get lit. I loved to be left alone on Sundays and watch football. I loved to sleep in till the middle of the day on my days off. I loved to read and work out. I loved to ride my motorcycle, spend money on myself. I loved expensive wine and good food."

"It sounds as if you kept living as a single man," Maria observed.

"Yeah, that was part of the problem," I said. "I don't think I ever grew up. I'm a little selfish. I didn't know how to be responsible for anyone other than myself."

"Didn't that change at all when you had a child?"

"When Nina came along, I was scared shitless," I admitted. "I mean, I was afraid to even hold her. She was so small and foreign to me at first. I didn't know the first thing about babies. I left that up to Caroline. Plus, in my defense, I thought I was havin' a boy. That's what the quack doctor told us. So you can imagine how shocked I was to see a girl.

"Before the delivery, I was conjurin' up all kinds of thoughts of havin' a son. You know, someone to carry on the family name, play sports with, teach how to drive—someone to have guy talk with. It's a whole different ball game with girls. You have to worry so much. I loved her, though, from the minute she came out, and I just figured I'd get more comfortable with her as time went on."

"How did that go?

Just then, I realized I had a follow-up appointment with my oncologist. I had to get my act together, and fast.

"Maria, I'm so sorry, but I have to be the one to cut it short this time." I explained that I had to get to the doctor.

"Well, certainly, don't let me stop you," she obliged. "May I just ask what course of action you are thinking of taking ... if any?"

"That's what today is all about, my friend. My options, if any, at this point," I answered. "Truth be told, I been so sick with this bronchitis that I don't know how much fight my body has in it. But we'll speak on Monday, and I'll let ya know what's what."

"That's fine. Good luck, Joey," she said. "I'll be wishing the best for you."

"I know. So long," I muttered before a racking cough began. I was feeling particularly unwell on this day. Figures it was the day I had to see the doc.

CHAPTER 19

CHARO AND I WERE LATE for the appointment. My penance was having to wait an exorbitantly long time in the dingy waiting room. I felt like I was getting sicker by the minute. I had dozed off in my chair by the time they called my name.

Charo gave me a nudge and helped me in to the exam room. The nurse took my vitals and drew blood, then escorted me down a long, bleak corridor for some X-rays. By the time I was settled back in the room to wait for the doc, my cough kicked up again, and I felt an enormous tightness in my chest. Whenever I stopped coughing, it took a minute for the sore feeling to go away. So when Dr. D finally walked in, I was ready to describe all my ailments.

"Hey, how's it going doc?" I asked.

"Wonderful," he replied.

He was a man of little conversation. I was used to him by now.

"So what are you thinking?" I asked. "Is it worth me trying to fight this thing?"

"It's always worth fighting," he answered. "But we have a little obstacle at the moment. You have pneumonia."

"You're shittin' me," I said. "Look, doc, it's probably just the bronchitis acting up."

"Not according to what I've observed. In addition, your white blood cell count is up. I want to admit you to the hospital for some fluids and immediate treatment. After a day or two there, we can pick up with the game plan."

"And just what should the game plan be?" I was curious. "How do we combat this thing without me feelin' like I'm already dead?"

"I'm going to look at your X-rays now and get a scan while you're in the hospital, and then we can discuss how to proceed. Right now, though, I want to get you admitted."

"Really, right now? Can I go home first and get some things?"

"Sure. I'll call everything in so when you get there you won't have to wait for a bed," he assured me.

So I left his office with my head and my hopes hung low. Just when I thought I might be able to muster a little energy to fight, I was being set back. Then the realization hit me. I was almost three months into my six-month sentence. I was no fool. I'd known people who were given a year and died after only a couple of months. I mean, for Christ's sake, I had cancer, and it was spreading. Every week was precious. If I was to be laid up in a hospital bed battling pneumonia for a week or two or more, it might be too late to fight. I might not get out of the hospital this time. Could this really be my fate?

When I arrived at the hospital alone, my assigned bed was on the oncology floor. What the hell? I questioned the nurse, but she assured me that because of my condition I would need special monitoring. I was still reeling to think about never getting out of this place, but I had to try to stay positive.

Charo told me she would come to see me every day, as many times as she could. I spoke to Joanne too. She was concerned, as always, but this time she tried to sound reassuring instead of making me nuts.

I had one request once I got settled into my room: to see Wanda. I missed her and wanted to tell her how it was going with Maria. I remembered I would have to tell Charo to inform Maria where I would be for the next couple of days.

I had found it hard to concentrate lately. My mind often wandered. Just now, I almost forgot where I was, and when I looked up, I saw a very robust-looking woman prepping to hook me up to an IV.

"Hello, I'm Pascal, your floor nurse this evening," she said. "How you gettin' along there?"

"Good, good," I answered quickly.

I just wanted to know if Wanda was in. I had to think about it for a minute before I could recall her last name.

"'Scuse me, do you happen to know if Wanda DuBois is working tonight?" I asked.

"Let me think who is she … does she work on this floor, sir?"

"I don't know." I had no idea where in this place she could be. "She's great, I'll tell ya that much. The patients on whatever floor she works on are lucky. You gotta know her. She has an accent kinda like you."

"Is she from Haiti?" the nurse asked.

"No, Jamaica," I answered. "She has glasses, and even though she's short, she's very strong. She's funny too."

"Oh yes, sir," Pascal said with a gleam. "Ha! You must mean Miss Wonder. We call her that around here because she works wonders for most all the patients she cares for. I can go find her for you, sir."

"Gee, thanks so much, sweetheart, I really appreciate it." I really did need a dose of Wanda right about then.

Even though I had been so agitated when I arrived, I found myself dozing off into a semi-conscious sleep. I could hear all the nurses chattering as they bustled up and down the linoleum-lined hallway. I heard monitors buzzing and other noisy hospital apparatus. Yet at the same time, I was dreaming. It was a crazy dream at that.

*   *   *

I was young and at the beach. I was walking, when all of a sudden I heard a car crash nearby. Most of the beachgoers got up to take a look, and some to rushed to help. For some reason, I could not even look in the direction of the crash. I immediately bent down and started frantically running my hands through the hot, dry sand. I was looking for something, I don't know what. To no avail I kept digging. I dug and dug until the sand was cool to the touch and filled with shells. Every time I lifted my hands, they were filled with shells and debris from the ocean. Nothing I touched was what I was searching for. And then the dream got even weirder, but I couldn't remember anything else.

My dreams had been getting stranger and stranger for a while. I didn't know if it was because I was on so much medicine, I was getting older, or I was dyin'. Maybe all of the above.

When I awoke I saw *someone* I had been searching for: Wanda.

"Hey there, Mr. Joey. How is my favorite Italian?" she asked as she gently put her hand on my shoulder.

"A, oh, Wanda. How ya doin'?" I asked in a groggy stupor. "I been lookin' for ya."

"So I heard," she said, leaning in to talk. "You lookin' good, sir, but a little tired. Maybe I should let you rest now. I come back later."

"No, no!" I perked up. "No, I mean, you gotta stay and chat a while. I wanna hear about all the excitement I've been missin' around here."

"You always were a funny one," she said. "There's nothin' funny 'bout this place. Although I do get some folks to laugh a little."

"So I heard," I agreed. "You are what they say you are, you know—a wonder woman. I always feel better when you're around. Look: you got me smiling, and I never smile. How else do you think I manage to stay wrinkle free?"

She tried to change the subject. "I don't know 'bout all that, sir, but tell me, how is it going with Maria?"

"Hey, thanks again for recommending me to her," I said. "She's a great kid. I really enjoy talking to her. She has a way about her. She gets me to open up. But more than that, she gets me thinkin' about stuff that happened. In a way, I'm reliving my life when I talk to her."

"I imagine that must be a hoot. This girl must get an earful," Wanda said, rolling her eyes.

"Oh, calm down," I said. "Don't get crazy with yourself. She's a lot younger than me. I try to watch my mouth a little—just a little."

We both laughed.

"But truthfully," I continued, "she's a down-to-earth-girl, and I feel I can tell her anything. She's like a therapist. She gets stuff outta me I thought I would never talk about again. What can I say, I like her."

"That is great to hear, Mr. Joey. So it sounds like this is workin' out nicely for both of you." She sounded pleased. "How are you holding up otherwise, dear?"

"I came down with pneumonia, you believe that shit? I feel like I'm being held together with tape and glue, to be honest with ya, Wanda. Some days I can't breathe, and I cough all damn day. It's fuckin' exhausting. But ya know, I don't wanna bore you with all my ailments. That's why I'm here, right—to get better?"

"That's right, sir, and you are not boring me," she said indignantly. "I wouldn't have asked if I didn't want to know. You are a tough guy. We can't have a case of pneumonia takin' ya down."

"You said it," I agreed. "I mean, listen to me talk. I sound like a monster. Gotta whisper most of the time 'cause my voice is so weak. I can't stay like this. I gotta beat this."

"I know you will give it your best, Mr. Joey."

With that, she was summoned away by another nurse.

"I'll keep botherin' you while you are here, don't you worry," she assured me.

"You, you're never a bother."

I barely got the words out before she turned to leave. I hoped she meant what she said and that she would be back to see me.

This place was so cold. My room was dark and dingy, with only the television hanging from one corner of the ceiling to keep me company. I was confined, and I hated nothing more than that. To get through this I would have to think of it as a vacation for my body to rest and get functional again. I would read the paper, do the crosswords, and get my memory primed for Maria's next call.

CHAPTER 20

WHEN MONDAY ARRIVED, I WOKE up with renewed enthusiasm. I hoped I would get to talk to Maria today; I had left very explicit instructions with Charo to tell her to call me here.

This place sucked, and I was glad to be feeling a little better today. Maybe the doc would have some good news and could cut me loose from here. All weekend my skin had been crawling, and I couldn't wait to get out.

At least Wanda was a good egg and kept her promise; she came to see me on her breaks, and we just talked and talked. Actually, she did most of the talking because of my voice. I learned a lot about her new granddaughter. She was beaming. She told me all about the things she liked to cook and her famous rum cake. She said she would make me one someday. For now, I was stuck with second-rate hospital slop.

Just then, Charo walked in.

"How ees my babee today?" she called as she practically galloped into the room in her stiletto boots. "Oh, *mi amore*, ju look so much better. Maybe ju come home today?"

"Hey, hon. I don't know what the doc has in store for me today."

"Ay, *Dios mio*, ju mean he has not been here yet? Where he is?"

"A, oh, what you bustin' my chops for?" I bristled. "You know doctors take their own sweet time. They figure once they got you here, you'll wait. It's not like I can go anywhere."

"Okay Joey, babee, ju want anyting? What can I get ju?" she asked in a babyish voice.

"Nah, I'm good." I answered. "Did you speak to Maria today?

"*Si*, Joey, she called just as I was walkin' out. I did just what ju told me, and I give her the number here. She gonna call ju later, babee."

Charo was a good egg in her own way. Sometimes she fucked things up because she didn't pay attention, and there was the language thing too. She didn't always understand what I was saying, but for the most part when I told her to do something, she gave it her best effort.

I was relieved she had gotten this right. I was looking forward to speaking with Maria. After all, I had nothing else to do here. So when she finally called, I was glad. Even though it was dinnertime at the hospital and the place was bustling, I didn't want to get interrupted.

"Hey there, Joey. So sorry to hear you're in the hospital," Maria sympathized. What put you there this time?"

"I got pneumonia, can you believe that shit?" I said. "The doc said maybe I can get out tomorrow. He's waiting for some test results. How you been, hon?"

"I've been really good. I was debating whether to call, because I didn't want to disturb you, but Charo made it clear that you wanted me to call. She's really something, that gal of yours. Quite a character."

"Yeah, yeah, she's quirky, but she takes good care of me," I said. "So what's on the agenda for today? I was thinking of some things from my days as an air traffic controller when I used to raise hell with the guys. Thought it would be funny stuff to include."

"Well, I think we'll get to that later," she suggested. "I think I want to pick up where we left off … with your daughter."

"You'll have to refresh my memory, hon," I said. "Not quite sure how we left it."

"Well, I'll refer to my notes. You said you loved her from the minute she was born, although you were shocked because you were planning on a boy. Do you remember that?"

"Vaguely." I tried to jog my memory. "Yes, it's coming back to me. It's funny how I can remember details from decades ago, but I can't remember things from just a couple days ago."

"You said you figured you'd get more comfortable with her as time went on," Maria prompted. "What did you mean by that?"

I paused to think about it.

"Gee, I was so excited to talk to you today, but I'm havin' trouble getting my thoughts together." I wanted to explain my silence. "I guess I just meant that, you know, as a man, when you have a baby, it's strange territory. So I figured as Nina grew up a little I would get used to takin' care of her and bein' around her. I wasn't used to kids at all. In fact, I grew up so fast, I hardly remember being a kid or even associating with other kids."

"I see. So it was hard for you to relate?"

"Exactly. I guess the mother has more of an instant bond, because of the whole giving-birth thing."

"So was there a turning point, or was it a gradual process?" Maria asked.

"For what?"

"You know, for getting closer with your daughter."

I guess she figured Nina and I had a regular father-daughter relationship.

"Look, hon, you have to understand something," I started. "Nina and I had a pretty average father-daughter relationship once she could start walking and talking. But it's not like the 'average' of today. In those days, men were not that active with the kids, at least not the men I knew. I figured we would just continue that way, but then her mother and I split, and it was hard for me to be totally involved. I tried to do the best I could. I know there were a lot of broken promises. I wasn't there at times I should have been. I fucked up. I didn't think much about it then, but now I feel terrible. Then I figured, as she became an adult we'd be more like buddies, but that didn't go so well either. What ya gonna do?"

"Oh, I see. But there must be some stories you could share about being a father or time you spent with her," Maria said brightly.

"Oh sure, I could tell you some stories, all right." One popped to mind right away. "This one is a pisser. You know, she was always a cute kid, but very shy and reserved. Her mother made her that way. Anyway, she must've been about five or six years old when I had my really bad motorcycle accident. I used to ride a Harley."

"This doesn't surprise me," Maria said.

"Well, I was a badass back then. I had wrecked before, but never like this. I had to crawl home from the parkway. I had a head wound, broken leg, broken ribs. I was a mess. Anyway, that cast was so itchy, and I had to angle a hanger in there to scratch my leg. So I was showin' her the cast, and I decided to cut it off and let my leg breathe. I was explainin' the injury to her, and all of a sudden, my leg bent where it wasn't supposed to bend, at the shin! Well, she let out a scream and went running. Her mother must have had a field day with that one. Ha!"

"And you find this amusing? I mean, wasn't the girl traumatized?"

"Look, when you're my child, you're in for a bumpy ride," I informed her. "That kid saw plenty. At least she didn't grow up naïve."

"I guess not. But what were some fun things you two did?"

"Caroline and I used to do everything with her together. We went to fun places like Storybook Village, little petting zoos, things like that. At first, when Caroline and I split, we still tried doing things together with Nina. But Nina and I still managed to do some pretty cool stuff together without Caroline. She was like my little traveling buddy. I loved to just get in the car and go on a long trip or a day trip. I took her to the mountains, the caverns, the Hamptons, all the local museums and amusement parks.

"Oh, we both loved going to Great Adventure," I remembered. "I used to trick her into going on all the crazy rides with me. She loved them once she was on them. She loved the Bronx Zoo—hell *we* loved the Bronx. It was different back then, not like today. We used to walk up and down the avenues and get fresh-baked bread and pastries and bring 'em back to my mother and father's house for Sunday dinner."

"That sounds nice. What was her favorite thing to do?" Maria asked.

"Gee, I never really asked her, but if I had to guess, I would say it was going to the City." I thought about Nina's smile when I would tell her we'd be spending the day in New York City. "Yeah, definitely the City. She loved it all. And we didn't even have to do anything big. She was happy just getting a hot pretzel from a vendor. In the winter, she'd be all bundled up with leg warmers, hat, gloves, scarf, heavy coat. All you could see were her eyes and nose, but she had to have a pretzel."

"Sounds like she just loved spending time with you there," Maria said.

"Geez, I guess. I mean I hope so." I said. "I know she thought of me as cool, at least during my PATCO days. I gave talks at her school on career day. She and her little friends would giggle and want to see my muscles. But seriously, you know, I was just doing the best I could back then. I had so much of my own shit going on. I had trouble sometimes just gettin' out of my own head. So I took her places I wanted to go or had to go. Sometimes I had to make stops along the way to the City to places you wouldn't ordinarily take a child."

"What do you mean?"

"Well, sometimes I had to stop off at a bar to take care of a little business," I said sheepishly. "I also had relatives who owned gas stations. After my days as an air traffic controller, I owned a gas station too … and these gas stations weren't in the most desirable neighborhoods, *capisce*?"

"And you had no reservations about taking her along?" she asked.

"Hey, whoa, nothin' was ever gonna happen as long as she was with me," I insisted. "That was for sure."

"She must have been pretty well-behaved to go along with you to all these places."

"Yeah, she was the best. I never, ever had to tell her to be quiet, sit down, behave, none of that shit. I was lucky. Back then I just took that for granted. She was an angel. She was a little too shy, though. Some days I could hardly get her to talk."

"So how did it go as she got older?" she asked.

"What do you mean?"

"Well, you know, dating and stuff like that," Maria said shyly.

"Ha, ha, if it were up to me, she would have never dated," I said. "Let me think … I guess I would have to say the subject of boys started as early as middle school. I remember because she was a little cheerleader, and some boy approached her at the field."

"What was that about?"

"What do you think?" I said indignantly. "The fuckin' mamaluke wanted to get into her pants!"

"Is that what you really think it's about at that young age?" she asked.

"Whaddaya, got your head in the clouds?" I couldn't believe the naïveté from such an intelligent girl. "That's what it's always about, at any age. At least it is for boys."

"Okay, well I respect your honesty," she said. "So did the boy escape unscathed?"

"Again, what do you think?" I answered. "This kid had the balls to talk to her, flirt with her, in front of me, her father! So I started questioning him. I asked him, 'Who the fuck you think you're talkin' to?' Then his voice changed, got a little high-pitched and he stuttered, 'Your daughter … sir.' I said, 'You're fuckin'-A right that's my daughter, and don't ever forget that.' I started getting louder and louder, and I wanted to know what he thought he was gonna *talk* to her about. Funny, he really had nothing to say then."

"And where was Nina during this scene?"

"She got called back to the field, so she missed most of it," I said. "She told me to be nice before she trotted off, and I told her, 'I always am.'"

"Wow, I can see why she may have wanted to stay away from you during her teen years."

"Don't get cute. She was a good kid, and I wanted to keep it that way. I had enough to deal with. I didn't need the headache of her getting into trouble. She never really gave me any until she was an adult, and by then she had moved away."

"Where did she go?"

"She moved to Florida with Caroline and her husband, Harry."

"Oh, so Caroline remarried. How did you feel about that?" Maria asked.

"Now, c'mon, you know you don't need that for your article." I was getting a little aggravated. I mean, how did she think I felt about it?

"Oh my gosh, if I stepped out of line, I am sorry," she apologized. "I just get so engrossed in your stories that I sometimes forget I'm writing this piece. Plus, I really feel like I have gotten to know you. I'm not a robot; it's only a natural reaction that I ask. You can understand that, right?"

"Yeah, yeah, I'm sorry I jumped down your throat, kid," I said. "Point taken. It's just that anyone in that situation would feel upset, regret. And that's how I felt."

"I see," she said solemnly.

"I had a girlfriend at the time, so I had moved on too," I added. "But I did miss Nina when she left. I knew I wouldn't be seein' her that much anymore. Again, as was the case with Caroline, I didn't know what I had until it was gone."

"So can you tell me how she caused you trouble?" Maria asked.

"Well the first sign of trouble was that she was dating older guys, in their twenties," I informed her. "Caroline would call and tell me she was worried this one guy was taking advantage of Nina. But what the hell did she want me to do? I was up here, and she was down there. One time I had to get on the phone with Caroline and tell her if she needed me to come down there and kick some ass, I would do it. That never happened. But then Nina came up here, as she did most summers, and things got heated."

"How so?" Maria asked.

"This is not a Cinderella story, so brace yourself," I said. "Let's keep it between us, *capisce*?"

"Of course."

"So she was up here for a while and had come by my job a couple of times," I started. "There was a mechanic who worked for me, and I saw him do a double take when he saw her. I told him what was what and to forget it. The problem was, I saw her do a double take as well. That night, she asked me about him. I told her to forget it too. She was nineteen, he was twenty-seven. I didn't even wanna think about it. But that didn't stop her. She came to work the next day and found out he played the drums in a band. He invited her to come see him play if I gave her permission."

"And did you say no?"

"Of course I said no," I answered. "But she was relentless. She couldn't let it go. She kept talkin' about him and how she thought he looked like a young Rod Stewart. I thought I was gonna throw up, listenin' to her gush over him. So finally I said I would have a talk with him about it first. She seemed satisfied with that."

"The guy must have been happy but scared," Maria guessed.

"You are so right," I answered. "I sat him down at work and told him that we had a little problem—that even though I told him to forget about it, Nina kept pushing the issue. I saw the guy start to smile, and I immediately squashed that. I said to him, 'Look, asshole, you take her out, get her home at a descent hour, and no foolin' around. Don't even think about gettin' cute with her, you understand?' I think he had serious apprehensions about going on the date after that."

"Well, you called him an asshole to start off with," Maria said.

"Oh, I called him worse than that my friend," I informed her. "'Scuse me a second, hon, they're bringing in my dinner....'"

I thanked the nurse who brought in my tray.

"This hospital food is for the birds, Maria. Anyway, I'll wrap it up. So they went on the date, for dinner, to a classy place. I told them both before they left that Nina had to be back by ten. That gave them tree hours together."

"You mean three?" Maria corrected me.

"Yeah, what are you, a wise guy?" I said. "You know what I mean. So meanwhile I made a little dinner for my lady and me. We threw back a bottle of wine too. It got pretty close to ten, and I expected to see them pull up any minute. Was gonna celebrate by doing a shot of sambuca with them. But ten o'clock passed. Then another ten minutes went by, and then another. So I did the shots myself, and I was pissed to no end. My blood was boiling. We didn't have cell phones then, so I had no idea what was going on. I went to my room to stew.

"Just then they pulled up, and my girlfriend went to the door. I could hear her telling them that I was in a 'bad way.' I came out of my room to face them, and I wanted to kill them both. I felt rage inside of me. They had blatantly disregarded my wishes, I felt. So Nina's smile went away the minute she saw me at the top of the stairs, and he could only apologize for being late. Nina immediately interrupted and said it was all her fault. She said they wanted to have dessert or some shit and the waiter took a long time."

"You didn't believe them?" Maria asked.

"Believe them or not, they didn't do what I fuckin' told them to do," I insisted. "And that mothafucka was supposed to have her home by ten! So I came downstairs and told him to come with me. He followed me into my room. My room was dark with dark shades, with very little light coming from a lamp on the floor near my bed. That's the way I liked it. I grabbed my knife off the old wooden dresser and pushed him up against the wall. I shoved my elbow into his throat and kept the knife in his sight. I told him, 'You see this, mothafucka? You don't fuck with my daughter and think you're gonna get away with that shit. What the fuck was going on that you couldn't get her here on time?' He said, 'Joey you got it all wrong, nothing was going on. What she said was true. I'm so sorry. I told her we should get going, but she promised it would be okay.' So I leaned in closer to his ear and said, 'Well, it's not fuckin' okay, dickhead. You disrespected me. Now you gotta deal with an irate father. To top it off, I warned you!'"

"So what did you do?" Maria asked.

"I scared the guy a little," I said, chuckling. He kept saying he was sorry. But I put the blade up to his face and told him that I'd hurt guys for a lot less. He started trembling. The pretty drummer boy was probably afraid I'd fuck up his face and then he'd get kicked out of the band. I pulled away and told him that because we worked together, this could get very awkward. I knew I had to get it together and settle it peacefully but still had to keep the upper hand. I told him that I wasn't gonna do anything as long as he didn't see Nina anymore. It was a done deal."

"Wow, how did she take that?" Maria asked.

"Nina never knew what happened, 'cause we walked out of the room with no problems," I explained. "But then I had to deal with her. That's when I found out she had a temper too. Once the guy left, she threw a fit. Screamin' at me about how I'd humiliated her. I told her I was sorry, but she didn't go for it. She kept interrupting me and telling me I didn't respect her as an adult, shit like that. She felt I wasn't mad out of concern for her safety, instead just because I thought they disobeyed. She was mostly right. If you don't command respect for yourself, who else is gonna do it? But now she was commanding respect for *herself*. It was that night I realized she was a grown woman."

"Good for you," Maria said. "And the guy?"

"She never saw him again."

"Hmm, I guess it was better that way."

I agreed.

It was time for my dinner, so I ended the conversation. We decided we would finish discussing Nina next time. I told her I really wanted to tell her about my days as an air traffic controller, and she agreed to write a little something about it. Those memories really stood out in my mind. I was looking forward to talking to talk to her tomorrow.

CHAPTER 21

THE NEXT DAY I AWOKE to the big head of the doctor in my face. He hadn't shown up the day before, so I wanted to know what the holdup was. I could be totally frank with the guy.

"So doc, what gives? Where you been?"

"And good morning to you, sir!" Dr. D said sarcastically. "I was called to consult on an emergency surgery. I missed all my patients yesterday. But I'm glad I waited a day for you, Joey."

"Hope that means I'm getting out of this joint."

"Unfortunately, not today. Your white blood cell count is up, and we may have to do a blood transfusion. And it appears that your voice is fading. Not sure if that is due to the pneumonia. I'm a little concerned. You'll be here for a better part of the week."

"You gotta be shittin' me!" I exclaimed. "I knew once I got in here you weren't lettin' me out. I'm miserable here. I gotta get out."

"Look, if we can get the ball rolling, I can get you the transfusion today, and perhaps I can let you go in a day or so. That's the best I can do. The rest is up to you and how your body responds. For now, look on the bright side: Nurse DuBois is working today. Maybe she will come see you."

So I signed all the papers he needed, and I got the transfusion that day. I rested, and shortly after that I felt ready to leave. I called Charo and told her to come get me. Within the hour I was outta there, without the doc's consent, of course. But I didn't care. It felt so good to walk outta there. I loved Wanda, but she would have to wait until next time to see me. And with my "condition" I knew there would be a next time.

I felt like a new man when I got home. I took a shower and cleaned up from that nasty cesspool of germs they called a healing facility. Things were looking up. I even got my call from Maria; of course it came later than usual, because she had to track me down.

"Hey, Joey. I was caught a little off guard when they told me you weren't at the hospital. You just up and left?" she asked.

"Look, kid, it was time to say adios to that place, *capisce*?"

"I hear what you're saying, but from what I can tell, you did things in an unorthodox manner. You know there are procedures to follow, usually for your safety and well-being."

"Yeah, well, you haven't known me that long, but can't you tell that I don't do rules too good? Besides, I am my own judge of how I feel, and I felt I was okay to leave," I assured her.

"I don't know, I still think you should have been evaluated," she argued. "In any case, at least you seem well enough to talk, and I would like to continue our sessions—even if it means tracking you down."

"Listen, sweetheart, I'm not that hard to find. I'll be one of three places: here in my apartment, the hospital, or dead."

I thought that was funny, but apparently she didn't. I could tell because of her stone silence. I knew I better say something and get back on track with her. "But yeah, let's continue. Where should we start?"

"Well how about finishing with Nina? I would really like to know how you get along in the present."

"First of all, you should know that we didn't talk for a couple of years," I informed her. "So just this past year I reached out to her, and we have been in touch ever since. She has a husband and a one year-old son, and she sounds happy. I'm happy for her."

"Wow, so you have a grandson. Have you met him?"

"Yeah, he's a real pisser. Funny as shit."

"They came here to see you?" she asked.

"Yeah, not too long ago. I know she came here to see me while I still had my faculties together. She wanted me to meet the kid. I got a real kick out of it. Who knows what I'll be like next time I see her. It was a good visit."

"It must have been hard for you to tell her about your illness."

"You have no idea. It was one of the hardest things I've ever had to do. I avoided it for a while. Then my sister let the cat outta the bag, and I had no choice but to deal with it. I know Nina is upset. I am too. I'm frustrated. I'm frustrated to think I can't move forward. I'll never be able to form a real relationship with her kid. I won't have the time to create a closer bond with her. I thought I would be able to make up for lost time. Now I'm outta time."

"I'm sorry to hear that, Joey," she said. "I guess you have to just make the most out of what you can today and be grateful for it."

"I guess you're right," I agreed.

"And your legacy will be passed on through Nina's child. I wonder if he will be a wild man like you."

"Yeah, that would be a riot. Too bad I won't be here to witness it. I'll tell ya one thing, if he is anything like me, he'll know how to take care of himself when push comes to shove."

"Why? How many fights have you been in? Maria wanted to know.

"As a kid, too many to count," I answered. "You have to remember, I grew up practically in the streets. My mother was too busy takin' care of little ones. I had to live with my aunt for a while, and she was crazy too. I was out and about on my own most days, especially as a teenager. I told you about that one fight during my time in the service too. I got in a lot of tangles here and there, but it wasn't until I was in my twenties that the real brawls started."

"Tell me about one," she urged.

"First you have to understand, I ran with a tough crowd," I started. "I knew a lot of 'made guys' and their henchmen. I had a tough guy rep from before I went into the service, so when I came back, I just picked up where I left off. It didn't matter to these guys what kind of job or status I had. I am full-blooded Italiano—Siciliano to be exact—so I was in. They trusted me, so if I could be useful to them in some way, you better believe they were gonna use me."

"Weren't you a little apprehensive about running with this type of crowd, especially after you got married and started a family?" she asked.

"No, sweetheart, my home life was one side of the coin, and my social life was on the complete other side." This was going to be hard to explain to Maria. Truth be told, I didn't know how much she would understand of this type of life, even if I explain it. As it was, only a dying generation of people could even relate to this lifestyle. Especially in the last decade, times were changing, and the way "business" was handled was very different. Plus, there were so many factions nowadays and wannabe mobs. Nothing was the same anymore.

"Maria, to be honest with you, this is a life that not many people understand," I tried to explain. "It was brutal at times, but it was very businesslike other times."

"What was in it for you?"

I pondered this question for a minute. I knew there was something in it for me back in my younger days, but now I had become older and sick. Life was long past me, and I didn't see any of those guys anymore. It was a damn shame. I knew some of them were dead or had disappeared, but where were my *paesanos* now? But boy, back then it was different. It was nice.

"Sweetheart, it had a lot of advantages and perks." I focused on the positive for her. "First of all, I got the best of everything. I had great furnishings, jewelry, clothes, great car, top-notch food and liquor. Wherever I went I had carte-blanche. I could take stuff that wasn't even for sale. If I wanted it, it was mine. You could be a *cafone* and not feel bad about it. Not only that, I had a camaraderie with these guys. We would sit and talk about things for hours. We'd commiserate about our troubles getting paid or threats or beatin's we had to follow through with. We'd carry on about our *goumadas* and our wives. We would start with wine and end up with black coffee and anisette to keep us awake. And while we were out at night, most people were sleeping. We owned the streets at night. And everyone knew each other in the neighborhood. If we didn't know you, fuhgeddaboutit, you'd better run the other way."

"So it was like a gangster brotherhood," Maria said jokingly.

If she only knew the half of it.

"So let me in on one of your famous fights," she requested.

"Oh yeah, back to that. You really want to hear this shit?" I asked, a little puzzled.

"Yeah, it's exciting in a way. So far removed from what I'm used to."

"There were a couple … It's hard to remember all the details now, but I'll tell ya about this one time at the football game," I started. "I rarely ever went to games. I mostly liked to watch them at home or down at the social hall or a bar. We all used to bet on the games. But this one guy, Tony Bo, was a top guy. Not a capo yet, but on his way. He got tickets to the Giants game and wanted to take me along. That's my team, man, so I was definitely in. Plus, nobody would dare say no to Tony Bo.

"In 1976, when Giants Stadium was finally opened, there was such excitement and hope for the team. They called four different stadiums home before that stadium was built, so this was a big deal. It was built in the middle of a swamp, but no one cared. People were tailgating everywhere."

"Sounds like a fun time," Maria said. "You've got to admit, they have great fans," she acknowledged.

"Hell yes, the best," I agreed. "So while I was at this game, during halftime some hippie-lookin' asshole decides to get cute. He bumps into Tony and knocks his drink over. It spilled all over his shoes. So I look over, and the guy says, ''Scuse me,' but not like he's sorry. I felt the guy had attitude. So I look over and go, 'What did you say?' The guy has the balls to say, 'I said 'scuse me, man, is there a problem?' So I look over at Tony, and he just shoots me a crazy look, and I know it's go time. So I whisper to Tony, 'Ooh-fah, I'm all over this mothafucka.'"

"Wow, the guy probably didn't realize what he was in for," Maria said.

"That's an understatement." I could feel my adrenaline rising as I retold the story.

"So I bit my tongue and bided my time, something I never did as a kid. At this point in my life I knew how to be a little more cunning, partly to cover my ass. This was crucial to be part of my crew. When halftime was just about over, the moron got up to take a leak. I gave Tony the nod, and then I followed the guy into the men's room.

"When I walked in, it was empty, 'cause the game was about to resume. He was at the urinal, and I darted right for him. He saw me coming and started pissing himself. As I grabbed his head, I said, 'I thought about it, and yeah, I do have a problem, mothafucka.' With that, I slammed his head into the fuckin' wall, punched him a couple of times, and broke his nose. Then I let him take a dirt nap. Ha, he deserved that! What a stupid asshole. Needless to say, Tony and I left immediately."

"That sounds awful … for the other guy," Maria said, chuckling a little. "This sounds like it was right out of a movie or something."

"Ha! It's real life, baby—" Suddenly I broke off, coughing. I had been trying to hold it back for a while, because once it started, it took forever to stop.

"You need a break?" Maria asked.

"Lemme get some water, hon." I could hardly get the words out.

Charo kept a pitcher of water on the table for me at all times, and I usually kept a glass of water by the bed. I took a sip, but that seemed to make it worse.

"Listen, Joey, why don't you rest," Maria urged. "You've had a busy day. Let's call it a day, and I will catch up with you tomorrow. Sound good?"

That Maria was smart. She always took my cues and let me off the hook just at the right times. She never made me feel embarrassed or awkward. She was kind.

"Uh huh," I muttered. "Sounds good."

CHAPTER 22

THE NEXT DAY MY THROAT was raw, and my cough was relentless. I had been feeling so good after that transfusion, and now I felt like I had the flu. How could this be? I didn't know if I was ever going to feel good again To make things worse, Dr. D had finally tracked me down—or should I say caught me. I made the mistake of answering the phone, and it was him on the other end. He was really pissed that I had checked myself out of the hospital and demanded that I meet him at the hospital. Once he heard how I sounded, he said he would have a bed waiting for me, whether I like it or not. Oh, goodie!

So once I arrived at the hospital, my home away from home, the admitting nurse told me to sit and wait. I waited and waited ... and then waited some more. Finally, the doctor showed, and after he made a brief stop at the admitting desk I asked him, "What gives?"

"Joey, I was with a patient who took a turn for the worse. The hospital is at capacity, and they were waiting to discharge a patient to get the room ready for you. I thought it would be ready by now. My apologies," Doctor D said with frustration at the situation.

"Why do I even need a room, doc?" I asked. "I'm not stayin'."

"After listening to you speak this morning, I knew I needed to see you for more than just a checkup. I fear your pneumonia is not gone, and your bronchitis is so bad that you hardly have a voice. Do you realize how you sound?"

Was this guy kidding me? Did he think I was totally soft in the head? Of course I knew how I sounded. What a prick. I felt like saying, "Just do your job, asshole, and get me better." I knew this would not go over well, so I held my tongue.

"Yo, doc, of course I do. Gimme a break here," I answered. "I feel like I'm never gonna get out of this place when I am here."

"Funny, that's how I feel about this place too." He briefly chuckled.

I wondered if he thought that was a joke. So I gave him a look and said, "Seriously, doc, I don't wanna die here."

He peered out from behind his glasses and stopped writing in his chart. "I understand. I'll do my best for you, Joey."

I had to take him for his word. Hopefully this glimmer of compassion was sincere. I also realized I better get Nina on the phone to update her on my condition. After getting settled in my first-class suite, I had a pleasant surprise: Wanda stopped by.

"Hello there, Mr. Joey! How are you doin' today, sir? I heard you were a bad boy this week. Of course, that didn't shock me," she said, smiling. "I came by your room, and to my surprise you were gone. I said, 'That's my bad boy for ya!'"

"Bad? Whaddaya mean, not me!" I answered coyly.

"C'mon now, man, did you lose your mind? I keep telling ya, you got to play by the rules here if you want the good desserts. You can't be payin' them no attention and checkin' yourself out of here."

"I know, Wanda. I was just really cravin' a hot dog and some Good & Plenty. You know those are my favorites. I just can't seem to get 'em here, so I had to blow this joint."

At this point, I was hooked up to an IV, and I could barely talk above a whisper. Wanda just leaned in closer and treated me like always.

"Look, I know you're just tryin' to get me into bed with you by making me lean in so close," she joked. "I have to work, but I will see you when my shift is over. You get some rest and stay put, man!"

"Will do," I promised.

A little while after she left, Dr. D walked in and delivered more bad news.

"Joey, it is imperative that you follow all the nurses' instructions. I have you under strict watch for your own good. You have a lot of fluid in your lungs, and quite simply, they are so diseased that it is hard for them to drain. You must not try to get up like before; you must rest in your bed."

"Whadda ya mean like before? I been here in this damn bed all day."

"Well, not really; right before you dozed off for a nap, you got up and tried to walk out … again. If you want me to make good on my promise, this cannot happen anymore. I need you to cooperate. Please."

Had I really done that? I didn't remember anything like that. Was he just screwin' around with me?

I told him I didn't remember anything of the sort, even the nap. "You must have me confused with some other guy. Or maybe you're just giving me a nice cocktail in this IV."

"Not really, mostly potassium," he answered. "Believe it or not, I'm trying my darndest to get you feeling better."

Before he left the room, I agreed to his requests. I had one request of my own: for him to call Maria and tell her to call me in the room. He assured me he would, but who knew when he would get around to it.

When he left the room I tried to regroup. I spoke to Charo, and of course the drama queen was in high gear. After every sentence she kept saying, "Please, Gods, help *mi amore* Joey, *ay Dios mios*, please … "

I had to keep telling her to calm down. She was so loud, too. I asked her to bring me some candy and to yet again tell Maria where to find me. Poor Maria, she would probably be glad to be done with me at the end of the week.

When the phone rang, I had a hunch it might be Maria. When I heard her voice on the other end, I was glad. She had a distinct sound and a hint of a New York accent. If that accent had been a little stronger, I would have sworn I was talking to my ex-girlfriend Patti.

"Joey Martino, you are a hard man to pin down!" she exclaimed. "Every day is a guessing game. Can you please pick a place and stay put for the rest of the week?"

"I'll do my best to oblige, sweetheart. You know, I gotta tell ya, you sound just like my ex," I said.

"Ex-what?" Maria asked.

"Whadda ya mean, 'ex-what?' My ex-girlfriend. Her name was Patti, and I was with her longer than anyone else. She and I lived together, too."

"Why not get married?" Maria asked.

"Well, I got together with her after Caroline and I split up," I explained. "For a long time I didn't know if Patti and I were just a fling and if I would get back together with Caroline. The relationship lasted over ten years. Relationships are complicated."

"She never asked?"

"To get married? No. She had been married. She gave up her dreams of veterinary school. She opted to work so her husband could finish school to be a CPA. Then the plan was for her to go back to school."

"So what happened?"

"Ha, what happened? A damn shame for Patti, that's what happened."

"The fuckin' guy turned out to be gay! He started his career and started screwin' around with some guy. Anyway, she walked in on them together, and she was in total shock. I mean, can you imagine? It's bad enough to find your husband with another woman, but a man? It was totally unexpected. She said once the smoke cleared, they had a long talk. He tried to repress his feelings for a long time, I guess. When she really sat down and thought about it, she said there were some signs, but nothing very obvious. I think she was looking for that perfect life. She wanted that more than she probably wanted him."

"How messed up for her!" Maria said. "I mean, it probably was great for the two of them to realize who they were as individuals, but how sad she gave up her dream for him."

"This is true, but they remained friends for a while, and he offered to pay for her to go to school, but she didn't feel right about taking the money. Anyway, she worked for a vet and eventually became his assistant. And of course, after she met me, she couldn't think about anything else."

"How did you guys meet?"

"She used to hang out at the bar where I usually went with my *paesanos*. It was called The Grotto. She looked a lot like Caroline, so I was immediately taken with her. But her demeanor was so different. She was more rugged and tough, kind of like Sharon. She was a lot of fun, in every way, if you know what I mean."

"Was she with you when you were an air traffic controller?" Maria asked, skipping over my last comment.

"Yes she was, but so was Caroline. I was newly married when I landed my first big job. I became head of my union chapter and was in charge of the TRACON. I was with Patti right at the end of the good years of work. When things started goin' south after Reagan came into power, she was in and out of my life. We broke up a lot because of all the turbulence in my job. I leaned on Caroline for advice during those years. That's when I could say we really connected on a friend level, and she was there for me."

"So even though things were not heading toward a reconciliation with her, you two were civilized?"

"Of course!" I said indignantly. "Why, do I seem uncivilized to you?"

"Not to me, however you do seem very territorial," Maria stated. "I just assumed she would have started dating or would have moved on by then. I find it hard to believe that you didn't mind."

"Now you're getting a little too close to your subject. I'm led to think this because you're making assumptions about me, a person you've never met. Besides, isn't that a no-no in your business?"

"In my line of work I find it necessary to make inferences even though I have to be objective," she retorted. "Then I can tailor my line of questions based on common sense or general knowledge. My question is broad and opens up your relationship with Caroline for discussion. As you stated before, relationships are complicated, so how did that work."

"How did what work?" I asked.

This Maria was good at getting information. I had wondered why she asked some of the questions she did. Even though she was clearly trying to defuse my curiosity and chalk it up to just "doing her job," I wondered what she really thought of me.

"Well," she began, "I mean, you and Caroline shared a life at one time, and you had a child. Then you were able to have such a friendly relationship? Didn't you want her back? If that were me, I would have tried to make things work. I think."

"That's right," I agreed. "You only think. You don't know. Nobody ever knows until they are actually in it."

I took a deep breath, trying not to cough in her ear. I wanted to take my time, because this was a conversation I wanted to finish.

"Sweetheart, let me explain it to you," I continued. "I loved Caroline with all my heart, but I screwed things up almost from the start. She always forgave me. I threw so much crap her way, and she kept taking it. Sometimes she fought with me, but she learned early on that I was a force to be reckoned with when I was angry or if I had a couple of drinks in me. Am I proud of that? Hell, no! But the goodness I saw in her sometimes made me angrier with her.

"Sometimes I thought she was sneaky, and I would accuse her of things. I don't know why. She was never up to no good. But then I would think to myself, *Don't be a schmuck, of course she's takin' extra money, of course she's flirtin' with guys, of course she's cheatin'.* But that really wasn't her. These thoughts would consume me, and I don't know why. Maybe because I knew *I* was up to no good. Many times I wanted to start over, but it only ended in an argument. As more time passed, there was more baggage. By the time things were going south with my job, I knew she had dated and I always had Patti to lean on. I'd go back and forth like a yo-yo.

"Then things changed a little. Patti was sick of my depressed moods, and I was making her crazy, so I needed to be on my own. Plus I was flying off from one meeting to the next, I never knew where I was gonna be. I always knew I could reach out to Caroline, plus we had Nina. We had to talk. Now, don't get me wrong. When Caroline started dating, I got major attitude with her, and I always made fun of her beaus. But I had no right to really fight with her. Besides, she was one of my biggest cheerleaders."

"Wow, even through the ups and downs," Maria said in amazement.

"Damn straight!" I said. "I don't know how much you remember about that time in our history. PATCO was our union, and I played a key role in the strike in the early '80s. I kept that strike effort at bay for a long time, until Reagan got into office and duped everyone. Then I had no choice but to strike. It was the worst time of my life. Something that was my biggest joy was coming to an end, and there was nothin' I could do to stop it. What a fuckin' waste. What ya gonna do?"

I couldn't continue to talk.

"It sounds like you took pride in your work," Maria said compassionately.

"You bet, kid," I answered in a whisper.

My voice was weak as it was, but it got even weaker, just thinking about losing my profession. I was filled with regret, anger, and sadness all at the same time. Suddenly, I felt speechless.

"It seems like such a noble profession. Very technical, I imagine," she said.

I found my voice again. "Yeah," I agreed. "And I loved it. I loved going to work. I felt powerful. I sat in a dark room, and that screen in front of me was my world. Caroline knew I loved it, lived it, breathed it, and she was proud of me for it."

"That must have been something, to know you have all those people's lives literally at the palms of your hands." Maria's voice was filled with excitement.

"Oh yeah, what a rush. Every time, too. That job never got boring for me," I told her. That was the truth too. "That job kept me on my toes. It's probably the reason why I drank and smoked so much at the time. Could be why I'm sick today. I drank so much caffeine and smoked so many packs of cigarettes during my shifts. I had to be focused at all times. There is no room for error in a job like that. For me it was especially rough, being the head of three main airport towers. I took my job very seriously."

"So that might explain why you felt the need to hang with your *paesanos* all the time," she assumed.

"Yo, whaddaya, a psychologist now?" I exclaimed. "Give a guy a break, will ya? I told ya, I loved those guys. Besides, all work and no play makes me a dull boy."

"Yeah, yeah," she said curtly.

"Truth be told, that job was stressful, and you are partly right; I did need to let off some steam after work. On any given night, at least one of the guys, if not all, were around, didn't matter what shift I worked. I think I felt like if I went out, then I wouldn't take the stress home with me. But sometimes it backfired."

"What does that mean?" Maria asked.

At this point my voice was very weak. I must have sounded scary to her. I didn't know if I could continue.

"L-li … listen, Maria, I'm getting tired, and my throat is really dry. Can you hear me okay?"

"Yes, Joey, I can make out everything, even when you start talking really low," she answered. "But I can tell you need to rest, so let's end it here for today. Tomorrow we'll pick up where we left off, okay?"

"I'm sure I'll be here, so you won't have to track me down at least," I said.

She laughed, and we said our good-byes. Just as she was about to hang up, I stopped her.

"You know, our conversations are coming to an end," I started. "I was wondering if it wouldn't be too much to ask if you could come visit one day. Jeez, I feel like you know me. I'd really like to meet you."

"That would be nice wouldn't it?" she said. "I'll tell you what, I'll come see you when we are through. Sound good?"

I agreed. Now I had something new to look forward to. I really wanted to meet this interesting girl who knew so much about my life—before it was too late. Two weeks worth of conversations were coming to a close ... and so was my life.

CHAPTER 23

"Mr. Joey, are you awake?" I heard a soft voice whisper.

I could barely make out the figure in my darkened room. She turned to walk away into the bright hallway, and I realized it was Wanda.

"Wanda, Wanda!" I struggled to call out. I felt as though I was shouting, but I wasn't. I could hardly get the words out loudly enough for her to hear me, but she did.

"Oh, Mr. Joey, you're up," she said, turning toward me. "I wasn't sure if it was too late to come by. Did you have a good day, sir?"

"*Cosi-cosi.* That means so-so in Italian," I said.

"Do you speak Italian, sir?"

"Just the dirty words," I joked. "I know enough to get by. It's really only useful so I can understand my old aunts and uncles when they talk about me behind my back."

She laughed. We always had a way of making each other laugh. This woman had become very special to me. She was the only good thing about this hospital. I should probably tell her.

"You know, Wanda, you're the best part of bein' here," I said. "I'd sign myself out and go die at home if it wasn't for you."

"Oh, Mr. Joey, don't talk like that! You haven't given up on me, have you?"

"I don't know, Wanda. Some days I got the fight in me, and other days I feel like throwin' in the towel. I'm just glad you haven't forgotten about me."

"Heck no, sir. How could I forget about you?" She leaned closer.

"I try not to show favoritism around here, but I'm truly partial to you. The trouble is, I think it shows."

"Ah, let everybody know!" I exclaimed. "Good, I hope all the other patients get jealous. Screw 'em."

"Now don't talk like that, man," she said sassily. "I know what it's like to be a favorite, you know that?"

"Really, how come?" I asked.

"Back in Jamaica, growin' up, I had a very good relationship with my father. I am one of seven kids, the youngest of the girls and I was his caretaker. He used to call me his pet. It always made me feel special."

"Are you kiddin', what are you, a dog?" I blurted out.

"No, man, it was a term of endearment. He used to kid with me all the time, you know, especially in the last years before he died. He got really frail and sick. I used to help him. He used to say, 'You know you are my pet,' and I would tell him to hush his mouth around the others, for fear their feelin's would get hurt. I'd tell him, 'Daddy, I know you love us all,' tryin' to be fair. I knew in my heart it was true, though."

"So now when I hear you in the hallway tellin' another poor bastard how much you care, I won't get jealous, because I'll know in my heart I'm your favorite, am I right?" I said coyly.

"You are correct, sir."

I fell into a deep sleep and woke up to a lot of chatter. I was used to seeing Joanne stop by and visit this week, and of course, nothing could keep Charo away. I kept telling them I would be getting outta here any day, but the fact that my sister was visiting more frequently had me concerned. They talked constantly while they were here, and I was used to it. But this morning I could detect a new voice in the mix. It was quite annoying. It was Angie, my brother Jay's wife.

"Hey there, Joe, how's it hangin', hon?" she asked in a thick New York accent.

This bitch annoyed the piss out of me. She played like she was my best friend, but we did nothing but argue. When I die, she will be one of those people who come out of the woodwork to commiserate over me with my family, because she flocks to melodrama. What a vulture.

She was my brother's partner in crime when it came to drugs. She eventually turned her focus to pills, mostly downers, and now she popped them like candy. She slurred her words in everyday conversation, and she didn't know when to shut up.

"Yeah, it's hangin', Ange." I could barely speak and I especially didn't want to waste my voice on her. "You good?"

"Not feelin' too good these days, but it's one day at a time, right, babe?" she bemoaned.

"Right," I answered. I thought, *One day at a time, really?* Who was she shittin'? This bitch lived in a beautiful house in the suburbs, drove a BMW, and wore designer clothes. She didn't have it so bad. My brother, on the other hand, was a different story. Poor bastard was still in jail.

"You hear from Jay?" I asked. I was trying to gauge her concern.

"I spoke to him last week..." she said slowly. "He may get out in a couple weeks.... I don't know anymore, it's too upsetting to talk about."

"Hopefully sooner than later, he's been in long enough."

"I miss him Joey." She started crying.

I couldn't tell whether she was genuine or just acting for my benefit. She had sucked this poor chump dry, and now she was crying over him. You know, come to think about it, he was probably in his glory being away from her. It was probably like a vacation, but without sex and good food. I didn't know about him, but not having to see this woman and fuck her would keep *me* in the can for a mighty long time. And now she was sitting here sobbing and staring at me, with makeup running all down her face. She looked like Alice Cooper. When was she going to leave? *Lord, take me now.*

"You know, I'm sorry I'm blubbering away like this. I must be depressing the shit outta you," she said. "I got to go take my pills, Joey, baby. I'll be back."

And with that she was gone. Didn't know if "I'll be back" meant in a few minutes, later that day, or whenever. With any luck, it meant never.

I spent most of the day in bed. I spent most of *all* of my days in bed. In fact, it had been weeks since I spent a day mostly out of bed. What could I do to get myself vertical again?

Then the phone rang, and it startled me as if a trombone had gone off next to my head.

It was Maria.

"Hey … hey there, hon," I said. "It's not like you to call so early."

"What do you mean?" she said. "Actually, I'm running late. Did you just wake up?"

"Yeah, but no, I'm up, I'm good." I tried to unscramble my head. I looked up at the clock, but I could barely make out the time. It looked like the small hand was on the four. Could it really be four o'clock? Had I really slept the whole day away? What was happening to me?

"Are you feeling up to our session today?" she asked.

"Yeah, no … I mean, of course. You just have to refresh my memory about what we were talkin' about."

"Okay, let's see … Yesterday you said that letting off steam sometimes backfired for you. What did you mean by that?"

"Well, sometimes I let off so much steam that I got into trouble. You know, it's a metaphor for the fact that I let too much crap come outta my mouth. I was a wiseguy, and when I had a beer or two, I'd get a little feisty. Basically, I didn't take any shit from anyone."

"So I am assuming you had some memorable moments," Maria said.

"Hell, yeah!" I exclaimed. "One time I even broke up a bar. But really, that had to do with Patti."

"Oh, here we go again," she lamented. "What happened, dare I ask?"

"I gotta think a minute," I said. I was really having trouble remembering. Events and places were sort of running into each other in my mind. "Well, let's just put it this way: Patti knew how to shoot her mouth off, too, and she knew how to flirt to make me jealous. I was a jealous bastard back then. Even with Caroline. Hell, one time I even put a gun up to Caroline when I thought she was cheatin' on me."

"Oh my, holy cow!" Maria shrieked. "Why are you telling me this, Joey?"

"C'mon, we're friends by now. Listen, I'm not proud of that. I don't think Caroline ever cheated on me, but back then I was crazy. I loved her, ya know."

She tried to redirect me. "But you were just talking about Patti." She sounded disappointed in me.

"Listen, Maria, have you ever been in love? Well, you're married so I know you know what it means to love someone. But I can hear judgment in your voice. Let me tell you, love is powerful, and it rears its head in lotsa different ways and brings up lotsa emotions. But have you ever felt like a good thing was slippin' through your fingers and there was nothing you could do about it? That's how I felt at the time. I had a good thing with Caroline, and I didn't want to lose it.

"After her, I went crazy. I lived like my true self. The wild side of me was in full bloom, and Patti was always along for the ride. Anyway, she made me crazy too, but she was more like me. Maybe that's why she was the only one to tame me for a while."

"Joey, let's stick with the story about the bar," Maria said. "I'm not judging you. Just entertain me."

"Happy to oblige," I said. "She and some of her girls had met me and some of the boys out at our stomping grounds. It was a very rustic-looking place. On the weekend they had a band, and there were tables where you could sit and eat. The action was mostly centered around the bar right in the middle of the place. It was my second bar stop after work on a Friday, and it was late, after hours. My after-hours crew were always my *paesanos*, not my work buddies. But I had my work clothes on. I had my collared shirt slightly unbuttoned, slacks, and I had to have my cowboy boots. Besides, these guys were always dressed to the nines. I couldn't be seen with them in a T-shirt and jeans. These were wiseguys. We looked the part, and nobody usually messed with us. There was Tony Bo, Ritchie Albano, and Luca "The Shark' Perillo, just to name a few."

"Why was Luca 'The Shark'?" she wanted to know.

"Did you ever hear the expression, 'card shark'? That's what he was, and he was ruthless. He got into every game he could and won most of the time. And if he didn't win, he'd find the guy afterward and take what he felt he deserved anyway."

"I get it," Maria said. "So how exactly did you break up the bar?"

"Oh yeah, so getting to that … Patti was there and lookin' good—a little too good, if you know what I mean. Her tits were hangin' out of her shirt, she had on a short skirt, it was ridiculous. So of course she attracted a lot of attention. This one asshole, who clearly wasn't a usual, decides to get cute with her. I give her a look across the room, then the asshole turns and gives *me* a look. I let it go. She walks over and reassures me that he was just innocently talking to her and he didn't know she was with someone. She goes back to her girls, 'cause

I'm with my guys discussin' things. A few minutes later, he gets a little closer to her. He wedges in between her and her friends and puts his hands on her, and I can tell she's uncomfortable. I walk over and ask if everything is okay. Now I can see the guy is piss drunk, and he mutters some shit about how he's just innocently conversing with the girls and he asks me if I have a problem."

"Oh, boy! It's on now. That poor guy," Maria said.

"I tell him, 'Yeah I got a problem, wiseguy. You're making my girl uncomfortable, so you need to conduct yourself right or step off.' So with a cigarette in my mouth, I slap some dollar bills down on the bar and say, 'Do yourself a favor and buy some other girl a drink.' Then I turn to walk away. I thought that was pretty civilized, under the circumstances. Just then I hear the guy say, 'Here's your drink, asshole!' and I can feel the glass breakin' over my head."

"My gosh, what did you do? I would never know how to handle myself in a situation like that."

"Yes you would. It's the simple fight-or-flight response," I explained to her. "You would fight and do what you had to do. I've learned that women fight their own battles, just not in barroom brawls. Women are more cunning and think about their next move. When push comes to shove, or when it comes to their children, I've seen it; they do what they need to do. You know I'm right."

"Yes, I guess you're right. I would do whatever I could to protect my child," she agreed.

"It's times like these you see what you're made of. But I already knew what I was made of. I grabbed a barstool in front of me and swung around and bashed him in the face with it. He fell back but got up again and came at me. Now Luca and Ritchie were on it, but then so were some other guys. Turns out this asshole who started it all was part of a renegade gang from Yonkers. We were all fighting, throwin' guys down. One guy started beatin' me with a chair until I fell, and he started kickin' me. I kicked him off me and pulled myself up. By now the whole bar was fighting, it seemed, in our little corner. I reached into my pocket and put on my brass knuckles and put a pounding on this guy. I saw Tony take out his gun and start pistol-whipping some other guy. Then glass and bottles started flyin' around, and next thing I knew, I was getting my hand smashed to bits by a guy slammin' a chair down on me. I reached up and got one good punch in the guy's face with my good hand and then I heard the police. At that point I passed out."

"What happened to you?" Maria asked.

"I was cut all over my head, and my hand was broken. I had a concussion and had to be taken to the hospital. To this day, I can't straighten out my first finger, because the glass severed a nerve. As for the bar, it had to close down for a while until the damage was repaired. Tony Bo made a handsome contribution on all our behalf. When it reopened, we returned like heroes."

"What a story," Maria said. "You have certainly lived a colorful life."

"I know—" I broke off choking. I was having trouble talking without coughing.

This went on for a few minutes. "Excuse me"—cough cough—"Let me get a drink, hon."

"No problem. Take your time, Joey." Her tone was comforting.

"Finally, maybe I can get a word out," I said after a few minutes. "These coughing fits are murder."

"You know, Joey, our two weeks is over tomorrow. I think we could probably wrap everything up now. Do you want me to ask my last couple of questions today? You can either answer me now or think about them and get back to me tomorrow."

"Go ahead—shoot."

"Well, I guess I just really want to know how you felt when you got your diagnosis. Did you fight back as you've done in so many other ways? And how do you want people to remember you?"

"Those are deep questions. Are you sure you want the answers?"

"Yes, I'd like to know," she said somberly. "I will most likely include some of your response. I know it will help someone."

"Sure, kid, I'll shoot it straight. I got one request, though …"

"What's that?" she asked.

"I'd like to give you the answers in person. Remember, we spoke about meeting? I think that would be a perfect way to end things."

"It's funny, but when you say that, it sounds so final. It's awful to know you are never going to talk to someone again."

There was silence for a minute, and then she spoke again.

"Our usual time?"

"Sounds good," I said.

CHAPTER 24

WHEN FRIDAY MORNING ARRIVED, I could hardly swallow, and I felt like someone was sitting on my chest. Instead of feeling better each day, I was feeling worse. I had terrible night sweats and even more terrible nightmares. Was I entering my descent into hell? If so, what was the catch? I thought all Catholic boys were forgiven for their sins and went to heaven. I might have to see a priest about this.

I wasn't going to let this get me down if I could help it. After all, I was going to meet Maria today. Just then, a friendly face smiled at me.

"Mr. Joey, my dear. How are you doing today, sir?" Wanda asked kindly.

"I'm better now!"

"That's good news, because when I stopped in late last night, you were miserable."

I was puzzled. I couldn't remember her visiting me. Surely I'd never forget Wanda coming by.

"Did I talk to you?" I wanted to know.

"Sort of, but you were not makin' sense, and you were sweating very badly," she informed me. "I got your nurse for you, and we calmed you and got you cooled off so you could rest."

"Gee, I don't remember … but thank you. Thanks, Wanda, for lookin' out for me. I know I never did anything to deserve you. You are like my angel here on earth."

"Oh, Joey, please, man," she said bashfully. "I'm concerned for you. I know how it is."

At this point we both got quiet. I tried to look her in the eyes. I needed her to know I wanted her honesty, no pussyfooting.

"Will there be a lot of suffering?" I asked.

I almost felt as though I was referring to someone else. It was so surreal to think I was talking about myself dying.

"Sir, you will be taken care of, not to worry," she tried to reassure me. "I'll see to it. Your pain will be managed. I'm sorry to say it's the others who will suffer, the people who love you and care for you."

"Well, thank goodness there aren't too many of those!" I joked, hoping to lighten the mood a little.

"Oh, stop it! I for one am goin' ta miss you like crazy," she said indignantly. "But hey, there are no guarantees, right, sir? I could get hit by a car on my way home, and then it will be you missing me."

"Wanda, I miss you every time you walk out that door."

"You're sweet …" she trailed off. Then her voice brightened. "Ooh, speakin' of sweets, I almost forgot, I brought you some rum cake. It's in the fridge downstairs. I shall get it." She started for the door.

"Wait, Wanda, bring it later, will you?" I asked. "I'm having trouble swallowing right now. Besides, I'm havin' a special visitor later, and I'd love to share a piece with her and tell her all about you."

"And who might that be? Should I be jealous?" she asked playfully.

"I don't know. You introduced me to her over the phone. It's Maria," I announced. "We're finishing up, and I thought it might be nice to meet her in person. After all, it's been two weeks now; we're practically going steady!"

Wanda's eyes got big.

"Really! Today you will *meet* her? How about that? She's lovely, your kind of girl. You're going to love her! And no worries, I will have the cake here for you by then."

Wanda was the best.

Charo said she would come by for lunch, and I knew she would help me get cleaned up and dressed. She was as good as any of the nurses, and she doted on my every need.

I felt like a nervous teenager. I couldn't believe I even gave a shit about meeting Maria. I guess it was just that I told her so much personal shit. This person knew my deep feelings, events that shaped my life, and whether she was doing a job or not, nobody had ever cared to know so much. And I liked her. She was familiar. I felt compelled to meet her and speak to her one last time.

I dozed off into a sleep. When Charo's loud voice woke me, it felt as if I had been sleeping for an eternity.

"Joey, babee, here I am, *mi amore*," she announced. Yoanna and I are here to help ju get ready to meet Maria."

"You two came here together?" I was stunned that my sister could deal with Charo's yapping for the whole car ride to the hospital.

"Of course, why ju look amazed? She es *mi amiga*. Don't be so silly, Joey, babee."

And with that, the two new best buddies clipped my toenails and fingernails, cleaned my face, and made the fuzz on my head look presentable. With the help of a nurse, they were able to sit me up and get me dressed. I was weak, and the clothes I had worn a week ago hung off me as I was losing weight rapidly. What a way to have to meet someone for the first time.

I was really impressed with Charo and Joanne. No matter how screwed up I had acted toward them in the past, they seemed determined to make this one last thing that was exciting in my life special for me. I really appreciated that.

When they were done, they left to get some coffee together and said they would return. Perhaps they would catch a glimpse of Maria. She should be here soon, and I was thinking about her questions. I wanted to be prepared.

She wanted to know how I felt about finding out I had cancer. Kind of a stupid question, I thought. I mean, how was one supposed to feel about the grim news of imminent death. I was not shocked, but I was devastated all at the same time. I knew the kind of life I had led, but could it really have led to this? And then Maria wanted to know about this fight, my biggest fight of all—and I had hardly fought back. What a chump. Would that be how I was remembered?

I was depressing myself. I had to stop thinking and just focus on meeting her. Maybe we would talk about the old neighborhood. That would be great. She probably knew many of the places I did. That would probably be the best conversation to have with her. Maybe I would ask her the questions this time, find out more about her and let her do the talking. I wondered what she looked like. I imagined a somewhat attractive girl, conservative in her manner and dress. Maybe she'd have brown eyes, dark hair, glasses....

It was almost time for my visitor to arrive when Wanda breezed in with the cake she had promised. She brought two cups of hot tea and set them on the table beside me.

"Hey there, is it tea time in Jamaica, mon?" I asked.

"Not for us, sir. I brought this for you and your guest. I think she is here. I could have sworn I heard a girl say her name was Maria as I passed the registration desk," Wanda said breathlessly.

"What did she look like?" I asked eagerly.

"I couldn't tell, sir. Her back was to me."

"So, you gonna help me greet her?" I asked.

"No, sir, I just wanted to make sure you had all the niceties for her that you wanted."

"And then some," I added. "Could you just do me one more favor? Jeez, I really hate to meet her in bed like this. Can you help me get into my chair so I can feel civilized?"

"It will be my pleasure," Wanda said.

With a gentle touch yet firm grip, she helped me get some dignity back by assisting me into the chair. Then she was gone.

CHAPTER 25

I FELT MY HEART RACING. Any minute Maria would be walking down this hallway and into my room. I wonder if she'd smell good. What kind of perfume would she be wearing? I didn't know why I was so interested, but yet I couldn't wait. I actually felt alive and well for the first time in weeks.

All of a sudden, I heard something amid the hustle and bustle of the nurses' station. It was as though my hearing had gotten much stronger as my vision and my body weakened. I heard the clickety-clack of high-heeled shoes coming down the hallway. It must be her. I was so excited to finally meet her. I wished Nina were here to meet her too. I had a feeling they would really like each other. Nina was a good kid too.

Just then I heard her knock on the door, and when she appeared, I was confused. Could this be right? Or maybe coincidence? My gut told me this was no coincidence. Somewhere deep inside, could I have been hoping for this?

"Hey, what are you doing here?" I asked, unsure of myself.

"Well, this is our usual time, isn't it?"

"You've got to be shittin' me," I said weakly. I sat back, realizing what had taken place. What did this mean? Hell, at this point, I didn't care. I was just so happy to see her. A flood of emotions came over me as a tear fell down my face. I could see her welling up too.

"It was you all along, wasn't it?" I asked. "Isn't that something? I'm glad it's you ... Nina.

With tears in her eyes, she answered, "It was me, Dad. I had to do it this way."

It was her all along. I couldn't believe this.

"Is it okay to give you a hug?" she asked.

"Of course, get over here!" I commanded.

We embraced and sobbed for a minute.

"You crazy kid. What did you do this for? I mean, why?" I wanted to know.

"Because I needed answers," she said.

"To what? I would've told you anything you wanted to know."

"No, that's not true. You would've held back because I'm your daughter," she insisted. "Besides, what great stories I have to tell my son."

We both laughed at that. My mind was reeling, trying to think of all the things I had told her over the last two weeks.

"See, I told you I was a good journalist."

"I see that," I answered. "I thought that now that you're a mom, you were done with that, but I guess it's part of who you are. So I guess putting yourself through college was a good thing."

"Could've used some help, though," she quipped.

"You done good, kid," I said as I put my fist up against her chin. It was a sign of affection. Suddenly, I thought of something. "Don't know how I didn't recognize your voice, though," I added, puzzled.

"Just made it an octave deeper, among other tricks," she said.

After we hugged, I realized all the things I had revealed to her over the last two weeks. I felt a little embarrassed. How had this changed her opinion of me?

"So, Nina, I know I've told you a little about Wanda, but I would like you to meet her."

"Um, I actually would love to meet her in person, but I feel I've gotten to know her already," she began. "How do you think I was able to pull this off?"

"You're kiddin' me!" I started to realize what she was talking about. "You called her to set it all up?"

"Yes, and she was very gracious to help me," Nina said. "I could hear in your voice how much you admired and trusted her, so I sought her out. She told me she normally wouldn't tell a fib, but since it was for a good cause, she was happy to do it. I really like her."

"Well that's good, 'cause I really like you too, missy," Wanda said as she walked into the room. "You have a great girl here, Joey. It's not many people who would stop at nothing to build a relationship with their ailing parent."

"I know, it's true," I said. "I really can't believe you both are here. Two of my favorite people, together with me for the first time. This is special. Let's have that cake, Wanda!"

It was great to see Wanda and Nina getting to know each other. They were laughing and joking, mostly about me, but we had a great afternoon. Joanne and Charo knew what Nina had been up to also, and they joined us. We all talked for what seemed like hours; it felt like a party in my room. I didn't like the fact that they had all kept me in the dark for two weeks, but I knew that this was important to Nina.

I still needed to speak to her alone to find out how she was feeling about everything and to answer her last few questions. After everyone finally left, I was very weak and needed to sleep. When I woke hours later, I still felt the need to talk to Nina. I summoned the nurse to help me dial.

"Hello, Nina, are you up?" I asked. "I am ready to give you answers."

"Okay, I'm ready," she said.

"First, I want to tell you I'm not too thrilled with the way you got this information from me over the past two weeks. You did it under false pretenses. I can't help but feel a little violated."

"You have to understand that I wanted to know things. Sometimes my memory of how you were when I was a child is a little foggy. I wanted to know that I had the stories right, especially the ones other people told me. I also wanted to know your point of view. Some of your stories actually made you more human to me. I got to hear real emotions and know that real-life circumstances have shaped who you are—that you're not just a stone. I hope you won't hold it against me."

She sighed. "Let's face it. I know this is it for us. I'm grabbing at straws to know you so I can understand myself better and keep your memory alive. Or do you just want it to all end with you?"

"Hey, whoa, don't get so defensive," I answered. "I'm having a hard enough time coming to terms with this. I'm foggy myself and don't know which way is up anymore. You have no idea what this feels like. I'm fightin' for my life right now. But now it's my turn to know things. I want to know how everything I've told you has affected you.

Look, I know I was a shitty father. I apologize, truly. Do you hate me for how I was?"

She paused for a long while.

"I know you're mad at how I got all this information, but you shouldn't be," Nina finally said. "This allowed me to see another side of you and learn how you felt about things, about me. I know now that most of how you acted was out of fear, not because you didn't love me. Because of that, I *can* forgive you now."

When she said those words, I felt a sense of redemption. It was like a weight had been lifted from my heart. It didn't negate my remorse or embarrassment for my actions, but I knew whatever damage was done, at least she forgave me. A tear ran down my face, and I felt its salty sting as it hit my lips. I sniffled slightly and then heard her sniffle too.

She asked if I was okay. All I could answer was, "Thank you. Thank you for forgiving me."

She deserved for me to answer her last couple of questions.

I took a deep breath and said, "I called you because I wanted to tell you how I felt when I got diagnosed. At first I thought that was a stupid question. I still kind of do, but the diagnosis was sobering for me. I'll tell ya, I thought I was going to either live forever or go out quick in an accident or somethin'. Never thought a disease would get me."

"Why not? You abused yourself for so long, and you're not a stupid person. You certainly knew all the health ramifications. You were reckless. I feel like you committed a slow suicide."

She said this with deep hurt and anger in her voice, as if I did this to her. I needed to make her understand I never meant to hurt or disappoint her.

"Yeah, but I felt I counterbalanced a lot of that with my working out. But none of that matters now. Was I a selfish fool? Yeah. Did I have good times? Yeah. Am I payin' for it now? Of course. Do I regret I won't be around to live life and see you anymore? You bet I do.

"For so many years I thought the world would be better off without me. I wanted to die so badly and end the turmoil in my life … and that was cowardly. I know that now. And now actually facin' death, I wanna live. Pretty ironic. But the bottom line is, when I got the diagnosis, I scratched my head to try to make sense of it. In the end, it is what it is."

"So that's it?" she said. "Does that mean that when you said you would look into more treatment, you were lying? Did you have any intention of doing that? Was this your attitude the whole way through?"

"No, I really did have hope when we first did treatment," I answered. "In answer to your second question, I really did fight back. I mean, my God Nina, you heard me on the floor while I was delusional and shaking from fever and throwin' up. You know how hard some of this has been. Just walk in my shoes for a minute. I'm past the point of getting better. I had hoped this last trip to the hospital would not be my last, but now I know it is. I just have one request: I don't wanna fuckin' die here."

At that point I couldn't think straight. I had gotten myself so worked up that I began to cough, and I couldn't catch my breath. I dropped the phone, and soon a nurse came in to hang it up and tend to me. I knew I would see Nina in the morning, and I hoped we would get to her last question.

Nina was at my bedside bright and early to greet me when I woke up. She seemed a little remorseful for taking a defensive tone with me at times the day before. She was like me: despite the tough exterior, stuff really bothered her on the inside.

We made some small talk, but I could hardly speak. As she held my hand, she assured me she wouldn't let me die in this place. My lips felt pasted together, and she kept moistening them with a wet cloth. She knelt closer to my ear and said words I hadn't heard in I don't remember when.

"I love you; please remember that."

I could tell she meant what she said, and it was like beautiful music. I didn't know if I deserved this from her, but I savored it. I nodded and told her I loved her too. Before she had arrived that day I felt myself slipping away, but I knew I had to pull myself together for her. It was all worth the struggle to stay in this world to hear those words from her.

I thought to myself about her last question. I really didn't want to be remembered this way, that's for sure.

"You know, Neen, I always used to say to you, 'Don't grow up to be like me,' right?"

"Sure I remember," she said lovingly.

"I meant that in regards to all my weaknesses. I would never admit this before, but I was weak. I gave in to all my impulses. I didn't have any willpower to do the right things for my own good. You were right when you said I had fear. I was afraid to face the hard stuff and do the right thing. I just lived for instant gratification. Where did that get me? Nowhere, that's where."

"You had so much ability, talent, and love deep inside you. I will remember that about you, and not just the crazy, impulsive you," Nina interjected. "Other people will remember that about you, too."

"It was wasted talent," Joey said. "If I had only known then what I know now, right?"

"I guess the lesson is right there," she said. "I guess each one of us has a talent, and sometimes you follow that path, and sometimes you don't. The key is having the courage to follow it, I guess. That's what I am going to teach my son."

"Good advice. I hope it sticks," I said.

As I said that, I pondered what my life could've been if someone had taught me that lesson from the beginning. My grandson was a lucky son of a gun. I could die in peace knowing he was in good hands with Nina as his mother. I was in good hands, too.

CHAPTER 26

NINA

HOW COULD THIS BE HAPPENING? I thought I would have a few more months with Joey, but this was it. Joey and I were saying our good-byes.

As I watched him struggling, gasping for air, panic started to set in.

"Joey, I want you to know me!" I felt like I was shouting even though I was sitting right by his ear. "You know, as I am now, a woman, not some timid little girl or a silly teenager. We are running out of time."

"I know you," he muttered.

"No, you don't, I'm not the same," I insisted.

He gazed over at me and focused on my eyes. "Yes you are, you're the same to me, and you'll always be that little girl." He paused, looked away, and then looked back at me.

"I'll see you again," he said.

Ugh! I wanted to scream. What did that mean? I couldn't ask him to expound on that comment. He could hardly get that much out. Was he talking crazy, or did he really believe that? God, I would like to believe that, but I didn't know what happened after death. Were we just balls of energy? Did we go straight to heaven? Was there even a heaven? Did we get reincarnated?

I wanted to just shake him and punch him. I mean, how could he have smoked and abused himself for so many years? How selfish. Or would living differently have even made a difference? My internal hysteria was getting the best of me. I had to compose myself, and fast, before he read this on my face.

He fell into a deep sleep for a while, then awakened and seemed very serene. He gazed at me and said, "You being Maria was not only a way for you to get to know more about me, but I got to know more about you. I do know you as you are now. Thank you for that."

The role of daughter was now out the window. I would become a caretaker, a sort of nurse-mother to this man. It was either that or walk away completely. My choice would be to do the right thing, no matter what I thought of him as a person, and no matter how he treated me in the past. To walk away was not an option for me.

Days in the hospital were long. I split my time between watching over Joey and trying to move him into Hospice care. Joanne, Charo, Wanda, and I all knew the importance he placed on not dying in the hospital, even though he didn't even seem to realize where he was anymore. He barely even talked anymore, and when he did, it didn't make sense.

"Nina, Nina!" he shouted in a ghastly tone. "I need some food."

His eyes were rolling back in his head. Charo was rubbing his feet and smoothing cream on the rough patches. She just gave me a look as if to say, "Here we go again."

"I need a box of Good & Plenty. Then go down the corner and get me a hot dog. You know, how I like it," Joey commanded. "Get lots of sauerkraut. I also need a box of Good & Plenty. No, make that tree boxes. I gotta have the Good & Plenty."

"Okay, so that's one hot dog, lots of sauerkraut, and three boxes of Good & Plenty," I said, playing along with the insanity. "You got it."

I looked at Charo. She had tears in her eyes. I left the room momentarily. I had left my family to be here, and now my connection to Joey was gone. He was in another place already; there were only moments when he seemed to be conscious. I was just here for those moments and to help support everyone else. I felt very alone.

Just then a familiar figure walked toward me from the end of the gloomy hallway. It was Uncle Vinnie. I walked over to him and hugged him.

"You're here," I said. "I'm so happy you came."

"You better believe it!" he said, and I chuckled inside. He always said that. "How are you holding up?"

"I'm good," I said.

"Good, good." He paused.

We sat together for a while in the lobby downstairs, on a comfy bench surrounded by plants. The walls were adorned with canvas paintings and photographs of doctors. It felt like we were in someone's living room, a far cry from the cold and barren feeling of Joey's room just an elevator ride away. We made some small talk, and then there was silence. Part of me wondered what had made him come here. Then he spoke directly to me.

"You know if there wasn't a me, then there wouldn't be a you," he joked.

But I knew what he meant. He was the catalyst that had brought my mom and Joey together. Maybe he felt partially responsible for my existence.

"But you know it's okay to cry and let your emotions out," he went on. "You're going through something, as everyone whose life he touched will go through something, and the same goes for all of us when our times come ... and the circle continues. But how you handle this now is the key to how you will mentally cope with this in the future. You know, Nina, Joey was my friend first, before anything else, even if it was for a brief time. He was a decent guy then. I'm here to pay respect to that person and that period of time. People touch our lives in all sorts of ways. A person can be in your life for a long time and never hurt you. Meanwhile, another person may be in your life for a season, and break your heart. Sometimes you actually learn something from the suffering."

"Wow, where did that come from?" I asked. "That was deep. I'm impressed. I didn't know you had it in you. You're actually a bit of a softie."

"You better believe it! There's a lot of things would surprise you about me," he said. "Don't tell anybody. But seriously, I know you were unsure about being here, but me, your mother, Harry, Scott, we all think you're doing the right thing. And even that doesn't matter, because you're doing what you feel you need to do."

"Am I doing it because I feel it is morally right, or because I'm deeply sad?"

"Only you know that," Uncle Vin counseled. "Does it have to be one or the other? Maybe it's a little bit of both. It doesn't matter, because only you know how you feel when you're standing over his bed, watching him fade. In any case, I am here for you."

He held me tight. We sat there in silence for a few minutes and then started trading some Joey stories. Uncle Vin wanted to go in to see him and, I let them have some time alone while I got some coffee.

When I came back up, Uncle Vin and Charo were outside Joey's room looking concerned. Charo grabbed me and said, "Aye, *mi amore* Joey, he es so strong, *pero* I know he ees in so much pain. Ju gotta calm him. Go in there!"

I walked into the room and saw nurses over him, trying to stick another IV in him. Joey was writhing in pain, and he seemed to be hissing like a snake as he tried to speak. All kinds of medical equipment noises were sounding off around his bed. One of the nurses quickly asked me to help hold him down as she tried to stick a needle into his neck after an unsuccessful stab at his arm. He was bleeding and coughing and trying to talk all at the same time. His chest jumped up off the bed as she kept drilling the needle into his body. I had to look away in order to keep my composure. I started getting nauseated, feeling helpless and horrified at the same time.

Finally the nurse succeeded at what she needed to do. Joey didn't want me to leave, so I stood over his bed and thought about what Uncle Vin had said. I guessed my reasons for being there were a little bit of both: moral responsibility and emotion.

I noticed Joey had some dry, caked skin around his mouth, so I took a wet cloth and wiped it clean. Just then he opened his eyes a crack and said, "I'm sorry, after everything, you have to do this for me."

At that moment I knew how I felt. I wasn't there just because it was morally right. I was there, and I was sad, and I deeply cared. I answered him, "I don't *have* to do this, so don't be sorry. I'm here for you. I care about you."

The next day, Joey was transferred to Hospice. We were lucky to get him in, because it was two days before the Easter weekend, and a lot of the administrators were out of town. It was such a bright and restful place, not dingy like the hospital. The room was light blue, and the curtains had a pretty flower pattern. There was artwork, donated by an elementary school, on the wall, and cards and flowers on the dresser across from his bed. I was happy we could fulfill his request to get him here. I put a picture of Jack and myself by his bedside, and I kept a radio on, set to a station that played oldies from the '50s and '60s. I figured, if he could hear it, it would remind him of a happier time in is life.

Joey died the very next day. Charo and Joanne were by his side. When I got the call, I was silent. I knew to expect it, but yet I didn't expect it. That's the weird thing about losing someone who is sick. You spend so much time preparing, but you can never really be prepared.

It's kind of like being in line for takeoff on a runway. You anticipate taking off. The longer it takes, the more nervous you get, with a lump in your throat and knot in your stomach. Then you start to move, faster and faster, until you take off, and then you hear the landing gear folding into the metal of the plane. As the lights go on and you see that you're safely flying above the clouds, you can let your emotions go and, maybe, finally breathe a sigh of relief. But this respite is brief; the second part of your anxiety, the landing, is just around the corner.

For me, the second part was the funeral and eulogy.

CHAPTER 27

ON THE DAY OF THE funeral, I walked across the green lawn of the cemetery and smelled springtime. That was the nice thing about the North. You could *smell* the seasons. I could see the church.

Most of my family were there, and I knew some were waiting to hear from me. I had been pretty quiet these past few months until now. I lived so far away that many of the old-timers who hadn't seen me in a while had probably forgotten what I looked like. Some would be scrutinizing and others gossiping about me, but I didn't care.

My purpose up here had been to find out about a man who was once in my life. Not only had I found out who he was during different phases of his life, but I had also found out how he *felt* about things. Most people never know those details about their immediate family. We find out more about historical figures than we do our own relatives and loved ones. Maybe that's because no one writes about their lives. Maybe we should all write about our loved ones and ask them questions and really get to know them. Or maybe we should all at least keep a diary.

I contemplated this while I watched people file into the church. The last car pulled up, and I knew I should do what I came to do today.

As I turned and approached the church steps, the person getting out of the car yelled out to me.

"Hello, dear!" Wanda called.

My familiar friend and I greeted each other as she walked closer.

"I just have to say, I'm so happy you're here," I told her. "Joey would really have wanted you here. I thank God that you were in his life. I think you restored his faith in people."

"I don't know about all that, child," she started.

"No, really, it's true," I stopped her. I reached for her hand, and we hugged. When we separated, I saw a tear run down her face.

"He meant something to you, didn't he?" I asked.

She just nodded, and we walked into the church together.

I felt an unusual sense of calm as I approached the altar of the rather large and ornate Catholic Church. The room was dark, as only the altar seemed to be lit, like a Broadway theater. When I looked back, I could see the usual cast of characters, but I just put them out of my mind. I was the only one to speak today. I knew I better get it right.

I cleared my throat and began.

"I think I speak for everyone when I say that Joey was a man who lived life his way, on his terms. I asked him how he wanted to be remembered. He said he wanted to be remembered as a tough guy, a strong man, maybe a wild and crazy guy too. Some of you may think his life was sad and tragic, but in some ways he was so rich and so lucky. Many good people loved and cared for him. He just didn't know what to do with the love he had. He had so many talents and gifts to give, as we all do. I think the saddest thing was that he didn't get to utilize them to their fullest potential. He wasted his talents as he wasted his life.

"In the end, he was grateful to get to know me again, as I was him. I know in my heart the love and forgiveness I gave him actually allowed him to rest in peace. Healing took place between us. But I felt cheated that we didn't have longer. I will fulfill my promise to let him rest in the Florida sunshine, something he never got to realize in his life but wanted so badly.

"I think in his passing we could all learn some lessons. First, life is short. Don't waste your talents. Don't waste your love. Don't hide under false bravado because you are afraid to show your skin. Instead, do let your guard down and share your emotions. Give freely. Let those you love know you love them by your words, but most of all your actions. Don't waste another day, because you never know which day will be your last. I know it sounds like a cliché, but truly make the most of every day."

With those words, I left the church and returned home to the arms of my husband and son, who every day I show and tell that I love. They, along with Mom and Harry give me the unconditional love that every person on earth should know.

They all helped me grant Joey's wishes for his resting place. Joey got his final wish to be scattered in the southern seas. Through my love and forgiveness, he also got his redemption song.

As for me, I am trying to live by the lessons I learned and those words I said at the eulogy. I am working on finding and cultivating my other talents. In addition to loving life, I'm trying to live my life to its fullest ... because I never want to waste it.

The End

Discussion Questions:

Do the characters seem real and believable?

Can you relate to the characters' predicaments?

*To what extent do they remind you of
yourself or someone you know?*

Why do you think the main character was so guarded?

*How do the characters change or evolve throughout
the story? What events trigger the changes?*

*Did certain parts of the book make you
uncomfortable? If so, why did you feel that way?*

*Did this lead to a new understanding or
awareness of some aspect of your life?*

What aspects of the plot pulled you in?

How realistic was the characterization?

*Would you want to meet any of the
characters? Which ones?*

Did you like them? Dislike them?

*Did the change in the point of view give you insight into
the characters' personalities and motivations? How?*

*If any of the characters made a choice that had
moral implications, would you have made
the same decision? Why or why not?*

Made in the USA
Lexington, KY
18 December 2009